D0062846

Wandering Star

——★——

a novel by
J. M. G. Le Clézio

translated by C. Dickson
foreword by Adam Gopnik

CURBSTONE PRESS

A LANNAN TRANSLATION SELECTION
WITH SPECIAL THANKS TO PATRICK LANNAN AND
THE LANNAN FOUNDATION BOARD OF DIRECTORS

FIRST EDITION, 2004
NEW & EXPANDED EDITION, 2009

ISBN 978-1-931896-56-6

Printed in the United States on recycled paper by Sheridan Books
Cover design: Sara Eisenman
Cover photograph: Stephen Polanco

This book was published with the support of the
Connecticut Commission on Culture & Tourism,
Lannan Foundation, National Endowment for
the Arts, and donations from many individuals.
We are very grateful for all of their support.

The Library of Congress has cataloged the earlier edition as follows:

Le Clézio, J.-M. G. (Jean-Marie Gustave), 1940-
   [Etoile errante. English]
   Wandering star : a novel / by J.M.G. Le Clézio ; translated by
C. Dickson.— 1st ed.
   p. cm.
     ISBN-13: 978-1-931896-11-5 (pbk. : alk. paper)
     ISBN-10: 1-931896-11-9 (pbk. : alk. paper)
   I. Dickson, C. II. Title.
PQ2672.E25E7613 2004
843'.914—dc22   2004013695

published by
CURBSTONE PRESS   321 Jackson Street   Willimantic CT 06226
       phone: 860-423-5110   e-mail: info@curbstone.org
                        www.curbstone.org

FOREWORD
by Adam Gopnik

When J.M.G Le Clézio won the Nobel Prize in Literature in 2008, few Americans had heard his name or knew much about his writing. This was partly a reflection on the insularity of American criticism, and American publishing as well, not made better by some pettish complaints about the neglect of "our" boys (and girls). But it was partly because Le Clézio, without being at all obscure, is nonetheless a "difficult" writer, even for the French—not a hard writer to read, at all, but one whose preoccupations and point of view are so oddly original that it is easy to miss the point of what he is doing even when one is, so to speak, right on the edge of his rapier.

Difficult, not because his prose is too cryptic or strange—it has a classical and even poise and a smooth, at times almost murmuring, tenor—but because his vision of the world is an unusual mix of things: his cool, almost detached descriptive particularism exists alongside a universalist, moralizing preoccupation with the problem of violence. A child of the Second World War, his earliest memories are of a Canadian bomb falling with concussive horror on his family's hiding place in the Pyrenees—it is the child's experience of war, at once baffled and bemused, that attracts him. In a larger sense, the idea of watchfulness, of bearing witness rather than registering emotion, is at the heart of all he does and writes. His narrative voice withdraws and approaches at the same time—withdraws the novel from the fussy seat of judgment, and approaches life through the empathetic description of entire worlds. He is both a writer *engagé*, and a writer merely watching, and the mix of the two roles is what gives his work—as in this newly republished, double-eyed novel about two children coming to consciousness that is also a plea for peace in the Middle East—its tension and its tone. There is in all his work an odd mixture of placidity, exactitude, and calm, with stirrings of indignation and a cry of complaint just audible beneath—as though turning down the apparent volume of anger when treating a political subject is a way of allowing the real murmur of life to be heard.

Le Clézio is genuinely, not merely symbolically, a man of many cultures, places, and tribes. Utterly French but long resident in New Mexico, his knowledge of the outer margins of world literature—of Inuit poets who write in their own languages as well as of French Creole novelists and Pidgin bards—is astounding, and symptomatic of his investment in an idea of writing that is larger and fuller than the conventional French idea of a one-way path towards safety under the cupola. That internationalism is, perhaps, part of his respectability, and can at times make his lesser work sound like the narration of a UNICEF documentary. But at his best he is a writer who seeks out odd corners of literary craft not from conscientiousness but from real need—because he knows that all of us live in odd corners, often no longer capable of being seen as such.

This drive towards rendering in words what most of us think of as "non-experience" has been at the heart of what he has done from the beginning. He first became famous in

France as a very young man, when his 1964 novel *The Interrogation* shook the literary world in France and stole the Prix Renaudot—this in a country where literary prizes count. The key moment in that book occurs when the troubled narrator confronts a rat, and for a moment becomes the rat, in all its strange rattiness. A virtuoso performer, Le Clézio invests the world of the non-conscious, or at least of the non-thinking, with his particular kind of humanism. He is a humanist without the usual belief that human beings must always be placed at the center of existence. His ambition is to render the world in all its actuality—the world of dogs, and rocks, of animals and objects, terrain and *terroir* as much as terror. This actuality includes human experience and human fears but is not made for them, or much inclined to yield to them in every instance. By expanding our sympathies to include those parts of creation which have none, we create a humanism rooted not in pride but truth: we are in one sense no more than grains of sand on an indifferent beach, but grains with eyes to see the oceans.

And so in *Wandering Star*, this lovely story of two destinies, one Jewish and one Palestinian, he gives us the look and feel of places—mountains in France, deserts in Palestine, the weather in the world—along with, and with the same urgency as he gives its story. They are not conventional "background" or even "landscape," like the flat sets in a conventional nineteenth-century drama, but are full participants, common players, in the drama. In *Wandering Star,* landscape and history, nature and culture, intertwine in surprising ways. Esther, the novel's heroine— though this word perhaps overstates her centrality—is a young Jewish girl in hiding in a mountain village during the

Second World War; unlike most accounts of such experience, the sense of terror and fear is almost secondary to the way the environment feeds and strengthens the children. Le Clézio doesn't scant the risks faced by the adults, nor their heroism—but he states the plain truth that childhood for children is nature itself, the way things are, and can be, even in what seem like the worst of circumstances, neutral and nourishing as any nature is neutral and nourishing. After the war ends, Esther leaves to find peace in the newly created state of Israel, but, along the way, has a silent encounter with a Palestinian girl, Nejma, who is a refugee from that new state. The novel pivots to Nejma's point of view, and tells her parallel story of suffering and escape, lit once again by odd moments of pleasure and set against an equally neutral and nourishing desert landscape, once again a full player in the story rather than mere background to it.

At one level a plea for understanding between Israelis and Palestinians—rooted in the truth that in any human conflict two narratives intersect, each most often in silent ignorance of the other—the novel is also a case study in Le Clézio's own peculiar kind of humanism. That is one where the life of landscape and the constant low hum of existence—of children and animals, of cooking and sleeping—drains the usual melodrama from the novel's *mise-en-scène* and creates an atmosphere of something almost approaching serenity—a kind of Buddhist calm— over even the most contentious of moments. Le Clézio's calm will anger or annoy some readers. But it should not be mistaken for indifference. The sufferings of both of his heroines are realized, and deeply felt; but they are never turned into pawns in a game of moralizing chess. What interests him is the quiddity of their lives as lives, sensitive to experience in an environment they didn't make.

Le Clézio's literary models are apparent: Camus, whom he often cites, is his most obvious predecessor in the placement of enigmatic fable against unblinking sunlight; Saint-Exupéry, in another way, with his stoical sense of man's smallness and nature's size, and his gentle, intense tone, is another. But J. D. Salinger, who shares Le Clézio's sense of the centrality of childhood, and his almost Zen-like feeling for the small, seemingly inessential but "speaking" detail, is the writer whom Le Clézio, surprisingly, himself credits for having first given him a model.

There will be those, of course, who find that Le Clézio's refusal of the usual dramatic conventions, borrowed in part from those earlier masters, cheats their need for obvious moral resolutions—to see good people rewarded, bad people punished—and who will find his balanced view, not of just political strife but of the struggle for existence itself, unsatisfying. Other readers may find something cleansing, arresting, almost Darwinian, in a vision of a world where the life of things, objects, and animals, intersects so calmly with the sufferings and ambitions of humanity. That it *is* a vision—an original literary intuition rooted in an experience of the horrors of the twentieth century but always rejecting the rhetoric of violence, however enticing, for the poetry of actuality, however strange—is something that few readers of *Wandering Star* will come away doubting.

To the captured children

Estrella errante
Amor pasajero
Sigue tu camino
Por mares y tierras
Quebra tus cadenas
    (Peruvian song)

Wandering star
Transitory love
Follows your path
Through seas and lands
It breaks your chains
    (translated by
    Jack Hirschman)

Hélène

Saint-Martin-Vésubie, summer 1943

She knew that winter was over when she heard the sound of water. In winter, snow covered the village, the roofs of the houses and the fields were white. Icicles formed on the edges of the roofs. Then the sun started burning down, the snow melted, and water started trickling drop by drop from all the roofs, the joists, the tree branches, and all of the drops ran together forming rivulets, the rivulets ran into streams, and the water leapt joyously down all the streets in the village.

That sound of water might be her very first memory. She recalled the first winter in the mountains and the music of water in spring. When was that? She was walking between her mother and father down the village street, holding their hands. One arm was pulled higher because her father was so tall. And the water was running down on all sides, making that music, those whooshing, swishing, drumming sounds. Every time she remembered that she felt like laughing because it was a strange and gentle sound, like a caress. She was laughing then, walking between her mother and father, and the water in the gutters and the stream answered her, rippling, rushing.

Now, with the burning summer heat, the deep blue sky, her entire body was filled with a feeling of happiness that was almost frightening. More than anything, she loved the vast grassy slope that rose up toward the sky above the village. She didn't go all the way up to the top because everyone said there were vipers up there. She'd stroll a little way along the edge of the field, just far enough to feel the cool earth, the sharp blades against her lips. In places, the grass was so high she completely disappeared. She was thirteen years old and her name was Hélène Grève, but her father called her Esther.

School had closed in the beginning of June because the teacher, Mr. Seligman, had fallen ill. There was also old Heinrich Ferne who gave lessons in the morning, but he didn't want to come alone. For the children, the holidays that had begun were going to be quite long. They didn't know that for many of them the summer would end in death.

Every morning at dawn, they went out and didn't come back until lunchtime—in a rush—then left again to run in the fields or play in the narrow streets of the village with an old ball that had gone flat several times and been repaired with rubber bicycle patches.

In the beginning of summer most of the children were like little savages—sunbrowned faces, arms and legs, bits of grass tangled in their hair, torn, dirt-smudged clothes. Esther loved going out with the children every morning, in that mixed group of boys and girls, Jewish children and children from the village, all rowdy, tousled—Mr. Seligman's class. With them, she ran through the still-cool, narrow village streets, then across the large square, making dogs bark and old people sitting in the sun grumble. They followed the street with the stream down toward the river, cut through the fields to reach the cemetery. When the sun burned down hot, they bathed in the icy waters of the torrent. The boys stayed down below and the girls climbed up the torrent to hide behind the huge boulders. But they knew the boys came into the bushes to spy on them, they could hear their muffled snickering and they splashed water around haphazardly and let out shrill shrieks.

Esther was the wildest of them all with her black curly hair cropped short, her brown face, and when her mother saw her come home for lunch she said, "Hélène, you look like a gypsy!" That pleased her father and so he said her name in Spanish, "Estrellita, little star."

He was the one who'd first shown her the vast grassy fields high above the village, above the torrent. Still farther up began the road leading to the mountains, the dark forest of larches—but that was another world. Gasparini said that in winter there were wolves in the forest and if you listened at night, you could hear them howl far off in the distance. But as hard as she listened at night in her bed, Esther had never heard their howling, maybe because of the sound of the water that was constantly streaming down the middle of the street.

One day before summer her father took her to the mouth of the valley, the place where the river becomes a thin stream of water bounding from rock to rock. On each side of the valley the mountains rose, like the walls of a fortress, covered with forests. Her father pointed to the floor of the valley, to the chaotic crowd of mountains, and he said, "Italy is over that way." Esther tried to imagine what was on the other side of the mountains beyond. "Is it a long way to Italy?" Her father answered, "If you could fly like a bird, you'd be there this very evening. But for you, it's a long walk, maybe two days." She would like to have been a bird, to get there that very evening. After that, her father had never spoken of Italy again, or of anything that was on the other side of the mountains.

The Italians were never seen outside of the village. They lived at the Hotel Terminus, a big white building with green shutters right on the square. Most of the time they stayed in the hotel, in the large dining room on the ground floor, talking and playing cards. When the weather was fine, they went out into the square and walked up and down in groups of two or three, policemen and soldiers. Under their breaths, the children poked fun at their hats decorated with a cock feather. When Esther walked past the hotel with other girls, the carabinieri would joke around a little, mixing French words in with Italian. Once a day, the Jews had to line up in front of the hotel to be signed into the register and have their ration cards checked. Each time, Esther went with her mother and father. They walked into the large dim room. The carabinieri put one of the restaurant tables by the door and each person who went in gave his name so the officer could tick it off the list.

Even so, Esther's father didn't resent the Italians. He said they weren't mean like the Germans. One day, during a meeting in the kitchen at Esther's house, someone said something against the Italians, and her father got angry. "Keep quiet, they're the ones who saved us when Prefect Ribière gave the order to turn us over to the Germans." But he hardly ever spoke about the war, about any of that, he hardly ever said, "the Jews," because he didn't believe in religion and because he was a communist. When Mr. Seligman wanted to enroll Esther in religious studies where the Jewish children went every evening—the chalet high up in the village—her father refused. So then the other children made fun of her and they even said, *goy*, which means "heathen." They also said, "communist!" Esther fought with them. But her father didn't give in. He just said, "Let them be. They'll tire of it before you do." He was right, the children in Mr. Seligman's class forgot about it, they didn't say "heathen" or "communist" anymore. Anyway, there were other children who didn't go to religious studies, like Gasparini, or like Tristan, who was half English and whose mother was Italian, a pretty brunette who wore wide-brimmed hats.

Esther liked Mr. Heinrich Ferne very much because of the piano. He lived on the ground floor of an old, somewhat run-down villa just below the square, on the street that led down to the cemetery. It wasn't a pretty house, you might even say it was rather sinister, with its neglected garden overrun with acanthuses and the upstairs shutters always closed. When Mr. Ferne wasn't teaching at the school, he stayed shut up in his kitchen and played the piano. It was the only piano in the village and there might not have been another one in all the mountain villages as far as Nice and Monte Carlo. People said that when the Italians moved into the hotel, the captain of the carabinieri, whose name was Mondoloni and who loved music, wanted to put the piano in the dining room. But Mr. Ferne said, "You can take the piano, of course, because you are the victors. But know that I will never play for you there."

He played for no one. He lived alone in that dilapidated villa, and sometimes in the afternoon when she walked past, Esther heard the music spilling out the kitchen door. It was like the sound of streams in spring, a soft, light, fleeting sound that seemed to be coming from everywhere at once. Esther stopped in the street near the gate and listened. When it was over, she walked quickly away so he wouldn't see her. One day she'd mentioned the piano to her mother and her mother said that Mr. Ferne used to be a famous pianist, long ago in Vienna, before the war. He gave evening concerts attended by women in long gowns and men in black coats. When the Germans invaded Austria, they put all the Jews in prison and they took Mr. Ferne's wife away and he was able to escape. But ever since that day, he never wanted to play the piano for anyone. When he came to the village, he didn't have a piano. He found one for sale on the coast, he had it brought up in a truck, hidden under tarpaulins, and moved into his kitchen.

Now that she knew the story, Esther hardly dared go near the gate. She listened to the notes of music, the gentle streaming notes, and it seemed to her that there was something sad about it, something that made tears well up in her eyes.

On that particular afternoon it was hot and everything in the village seemed to be asleep. Esther walked over to Mr. Ferne's house. In the garden there was a tall mulberry tree. Using the gate, Esther pulled herself up onto the wall in the shade of the mulberry tree. Through the kitchen window, she saw Mr. Ferne's silhouette leaning over the piano. The ivory keys gleamed in the half-light. The notes slid smoothly out, hesitated, started up again, as if it were a language, as if Mr. Ferne wasn't really sure where to begin anymore. Esther peered into the kitchen as hard as she could until her eyes began to smart. Then the music truly began, it sprang from the piano all of a sudden and filled the entire house, the garden, and the street, it filled everything with its power, its order, and then it grew soft, mysterious. Now it was surging up, pouring out like the water in the streams, it went straight up to the sky, to the clouds, mixed with the light. It spilled over the mountains, went all the way to the source of the two torrents, it was as powerful as the river.

With her hands gripping the rusty gate, Esther listened

to Mr. Ferne's language. He didn't sound like the schoolteacher now. He was telling strange stories, stories she couldn't remember, like the stories in dreams. In them, people were free, there was no war, no Italians or Germans, nothing that could be frightening or stop life. And yet it was sad as well, and the music slowed down, questioning. At times everything tore apart, shattered. Then silence.

The music started up again, she listened to every phrase that came. Never had anything been so important, except maybe when her mother sang a song or her father read passages from her favorite books, like when Mr. Pickwick is sent to the London prison or when Nicolas Nickleby meets his uncle.

Esther pushed open the gate, crossed the garden. Without a sound, she went into the kitchen and walked over to the piano. She watched each ivory key sinking down with precision under the old man's nervous fingers; she listened closely to each phrase.

Suddenly Mr. Ferne stopped, and the silence grew heavy, threatening. Esther started to back away, but Mr. Ferne turned toward her. The light shone upon his white face with its strange little goat's beard.

He said, "What's your name?"

"Hélène," said Esther.

"Well, come in then."

As if it were as natural as could be, as if he knew the young girl.

Then he started playing again, without paying any attention to her. She listened to him, standing by the piano, not daring to breathe. Never had music seemed so beautiful to her. In the semi-darkness, the black piano blotted everything out. The long hands of the old man ran over the keys, stopped, started again. Sometimes Mr. Ferne looked through a pile of notebooks with mysterious names written on them.

Sonaten für Pianoforte
Von W. A Mozart

Czerny
Preliminary Studies in Finger Dexterity, op. 636

Beethoven
Sonaten, vol. II, par Moszkowski

Liszt
Klavierwerke, Band IV

Bach
Englische suiten, 4-6

He turned toward Esther, "Would you like to play?"

Esther looked at him, astonished.

"It's that I don't know how."

He shrugged his shoulders. "It doesn't matter. Try, watch what my fingers do."

He had her sit down on the bench next to him. He had a strange way of making his fingers run over the keys, like a thin, nervous animal.

Esther tried to imitate him, and to her great surprise she succeeded.

"You see? It's simple. Now the other hand."

He watched her hand, he seemed impatient.

"All right, you'll need to have lessons, you might be able to play. But it's a lot of work. Try the chords."

He put Esther's hands on the keyboard, spread out her

fingers. His own hands were long and slender, not the hands of an old man, but young, strong hands, with bulging veins. The sounds of chords sprang up, magically. Vibrated under the young girl's fingers, echoed deep within her.

"You'll have to learn how to read the notes. When you know how to do that, come back to see me."

Ever since then, Esther had gone back whenever she could get away in the afternoons. She pushed open the gate of the villa, went noiselessly into the kitchen while Mr. Ferne was playing. At some point, without turning his head, he would know she was there. He'd say, "Come in, sit down."

Esther sat down beside him on the bench and she watched the long hands running over the keyboard as if they themselves were creating the notes. It lasted such a long time that she forgot everything else, even where she was. Mr. Ferne showed her how to let her fingers run over the keys. On a sheet of white paper he had written some notes; he wanted her to sing them and play them at the same time. His eyes shone, his little goat's beard twitched. "You have a lovely voice, but I'm not sure if you'll really be able to play the piano." When she made a mistake, he got angry. "That's all for today, go away, leave me alone!" But he held her back by the arm, and for her he played one of Mozart's sonatas, the one he liked best. When Esther went out into the street, she was dazed by the sunlight and the silence; it took her a few minutes to get oriented again.

Late in the afternoon, Esther saw Mr. Ferne in the village square. People came up to greet him, and he talked about anything but music. They were rich people who lived in the chalets on the other side of the torrent, amid gardens where tall chestnut trees grew. Esther's father didn't like them much, but he wouldn't stand for anyone to speak ill of them because they helped the poor people who came from Russia or from Poland. Mr. Ferne greeted everyone ceremoniously, sharing a few words with each, then he went back to his run-down house.

Near evening the square livened up, people came from all the streets in Saint-Martin, wealthy people from the villas and the poor who lived in hotel rooms, farmers back from the war, village women in aprons, young girls walking in groups of three under the watchful eyes of the carabinieri and the Italian soldiers, diamond-dealers, tailors, furriers from northern Europe. Children ran across the square, laughing and bumping into the girls, or playing hide-and-seek behind the trees. Esther just sat on the low wall on the edge of the square, watching all the people. She listened to the sounds of voices, the calls, the shouts of children erupting suddenly like the squawking of birds.

Then the sun slipped behind the mountain and a sort of milky haze blurred the village. Shadows crept into the square. Everything seemed strange, far away. Esther thought of her father who was walking through the tall grass somewhere in the mountains, on the way back from his meeting. Elizabeth never came to the square, she waited at home, knitting with bits of yarn, trying not to worry. Esther just couldn't understand what it all meant, the men and the women, all so different, speaking all kinds of languages, coming from all over the world to this square. She watched the old Jews wearing their long black coats, the peasant women with their clothing worn thin from working in the fields, and the young girls circling the fountain in their pale-colored dresses.

When the light disappeared, the square slowly emptied. Everyone went back to their homes, the voices faded away one after the other. You could hear the gurgling of the fountain and the cries of children running after each other through the streets. Elizabeth walked into the square. She took Esther by the hand and they went down to the dark little apartment together. They walked in step, their shoes echoing in unison down the street. Esther liked that. She held her mother's hand very tightly; it was as if they were both thirteen years old, and had their whole lives in front of them.

Tristan could still remember his mother's hands playing the black piano in the afternoon when everything around seemed to be drowsing. In the living room there were sometimes guests, he heard voices, the laughter of his mother's friends. Tristan couldn't remember their names anymore. He only saw the movement of hands over the piano keys, and the music burst forth. That was very long ago. He didn't know when she'd told him the name of that music, *La Cathédrale engloutie*, with the sound of bells ringing under the sea. It was in Cannes, in another time, in another world. Then he wanted to go back to that life, as in a dream. The piano music swelled, filled the small hotel room, slipped out into the hallways, reaching every floor. It rang out loudly in the night silence. Tristan could hear his heart beating in rhythm with the music and suddenly he awoke from his dream, terrified, his back soaked with sweat; he sat up in his bed to listen, to make sure that no one else had heard the music. He listened to the peaceful breathing of his sleeping mother and, on the other side of the shutters, the sound of the water in the fountain.

They lived on the second floor of the Hotel Victoria, a small room with a balcony looking out over the square. All the floors were filled with poor families whom the Italians had put under house arrest, and there were so many people that in the daytime the hotel buzzed like a beehive. When Mrs. O'Rourke had arrived in Saint-Martin on the bus,

Tristan was a lonely, shy boy of twelve. His straight blond hair was trimmed around his head in a "bowl cut," he wore strange English clothes—gray flannel shorts that were too long, woolen stockings and odd-looking vests. Everything about him was foreign. In Cannes, they'd lived with a small circle of English expatriates in summer residences that the war had pared down even more. War had broken out and Tristan's father, who was a businessman in equatorial Africa, had enrolled in the colonial armed forces. Since then, they had no news of him. Tristan stopped going to school and his mother gave him lessons at home. And so, when they'd reached the mountains, Mrs. O'Rourke didn't want to enroll Tristan in Mr. Seligman's school. The first memory Esther had of him was his silhouette in strange clothing as he stood in the doorway of the hotel watching the children on their way to school.

Mrs. O'Rourke was beautiful. Her long dresses and wide-brimmed hats contrasted with her sober face, the slightly melancholy cast to her eyes. She spoke very pure French, with no accent, and people said she was a spy working for the carabinieri, or that she was a criminal in hiding. It was mostly the girls who whispered stories to each other. It was the same when they talked about Rachel, who was seeing the captain of the carabinieri in secret.

So at first Tristan didn't want to mix with the other children. He walked around the village alone, or sometimes he went out into the fields, walked down the slope till he reached the river. When he found other children there, he climbed back up without turning around. Maybe he was afraid of them. He wanted to show he didn't need anyone.

Evenings, Esther saw him walking around in the square, offering his arm ceremoniously to his mother. They strolled under the plane trees to the other end of the square where the carabinieri were. Then they turned and started back the other way. People didn't talk much with Mrs. O'Rourke. But she exchanged a few words with old Heinrich Ferne because he was a musician. She never went with the others to have her name checked on the list at the Hotel Terminus. She wasn't Jewish.

Time had passed, it was almost summer. Now everyone knew that Mrs. O'Rourke wasn't rich. They even said that she had no money at all, because she went to see the diamond dealers to borrow money in exchange for her jewelry. They said she hardly had anything left to pawn, just a few lockets, some ivory necklaces, some trinkets.

Tristan looked at his mother as if he'd never seen her before. He wanted to remember the days in the house in Cannes, the mimosas in the afternoon light, the birds singing outside, his mother's voice, and always the hands playing *La Cathédrale engloutie*, the music—so very brutal one minute, so very sad the next. The scene was getting blurry, drifting away.

Tristan couldn't bear it in the hotel room anymore. The sun had burned his face and hands, had bleached his hair that had grown too long. His clothes were ragged and dirty from running through the bushes. One day on the road leading out of the village, he'd gotten into a fight with Gasparini because the boy was flirting with Esther. Gasparini was older, stronger, and he'd put a neck-lock on Tristan; his face was contorted with hatred, he said, "Go ahead, say you're a jerk! Say it!" Tristan had held out till he fainted. In the end, Gasparini let go of him; he let the others think that Tristan had given in.

Ever since that day, everything had changed. Now it was summer, the days had grown long. Tristan left the hotel every morning while his mother still slept in the narrow room. He didn't come back till noon, starving, his legs scratched by brambles. His mother didn't say anything, but she had a pretty good idea. One day as he was going out, she said in an odd voice, "You know, Tristan, that young girl isn't for you." He stopped short. "What on earth are you talking about? What young girl?" She simply repeated, "She's not for you, Tristan." But she never brought it up again.

In the morning, Tristan was in the village square just when the Jews were lining up in front of the door to the Hotel Terminus. The men and women waited their turn to go in, to have their names checked off in the register, and receive their ration cards.

Half-hidden behind the trees, Tristan watched Esther and her parents as they waited. He was a little ashamed because he and his mother didn't have to stand in line; they weren't like the others. It was right there in that square that Esther had looked at him for the first time. It was raining off and on. The women wrapped themselves tightly in their shawls, opened their big black umbrellas. The children stayed close by, not running, not shouting. In the shade of the plane trees, Tristan watched Esther standing in the middle of the line. Her head was bare, drops of rain sparkled in her black hair. She was holding her mother's arm, and her father looked very tall next to her. She wasn't talking; no one was talking, not even the carabinieri standing in front of the door to the restaurant. Every time the door opened, Tristan caught a quick glimpse of the large room lit by the French doors thrown open onto the garden. The carabinieri were standing near the windows smoking. One of them was sitting at a table with an open register in front of him, he was checking off the names. For Tristan, there was something awful, something mysterious about it all, as if the people who went into the room wouldn't come out again. On the side of the hotel facing the square, the windows were closed, curtains drawn. When night fell, the Italians closed the shutters and barricaded themselves inside the hotel. The square was pitch-dark, as if uninhabited. No one was allowed to go out.

It was the silence that drew Tristan to the hotel. He'd left the tepid room where his mother was breathing softly, the dream of music and gardens, to come and watch Esther among all the dark shapes waiting in the square. The carabinieri wrote down her name. She went in with her mother and father, and the man with the register marked her name in the notebook, at the bottom of the list with all the other names. Tristan would have liked to be with her in the line, move up with her till they reached the table; he couldn't sleep in the room at the Hotel Victoria while that was happening. The silence in the square was too heavy. The only sound was that of the water in the basin of the fountain; a dog barked somewhere.

Afterward, Esther came back out. She walked in the square a little off to one side of her mother and father. When she went past the trees, she saw Tristan and there was a blaze in her black eyes, something like anger, or disdain, a violent flame that had made the boy's heart beat too fast. He stepped back. He wanted to say, you're beautiful, I can't think of anything but you, I love you. But the silhouettes were already hurrying off toward the narrow streets.

The sun rose in the sky, the light burned down between the clouds. In the fields, the grass was razor sharp, the bushes whipped at your legs. Tristan was running to get away, he went all the way down to the icy stream. The air was full of smells, of pollen, of flies.

It was as if there had never been a summer before that one. The sun scorched the grasses in the fields, the stones in the torrent, and the mountains seemed so distant against the dark blue sky. Esther often walked down to the river, deep in the valley, to the place where the two torrents met and the valley grew very wide. The circle of mountains seemed even more distant there. In the morning, the air was smooth and cold, the sky utterly blue. Then, after noon, clouds appeared above the peaks to the north and east, roiling up into bright billows. The light vibrated over the river water. The vibration was everywhere; when you turned your head, it merged with the sound of the water and the song of crickets.

One day, Gasparini came down to the river with Esther. When the sun was in mid-sky, Esther started to walk back up the slope toward home, and Gasparini took her hand.

"Come on, let's go down to see my cousin cutting the wheat in Roquebillière." Esther hesitated. "It's not far, just a little farther down, we'll go in my grandfather's cart," said Gasparini.

Esther had seen the harvest once, long ago, with her father, but she wasn't sure she remembered what the wheat looked like. In the end she climbed up into the cart. There were women with scarves on their heads, children. Old Grandfather Gasparini was leading the horse. The cart followed the curves of the track down into the valley. There were no more houses, only the river shimmering in the sunlight, the green fields. The track was rutted, the cart lurched to and fro and it made the women laugh. Shortly before reaching Roquebillière, the valley widened out. Before seeing anything, Esther heard sounds: shouts, women's voices, shrill laughter that floated over on the hot wind, and a rustling sound, soft and even, like the sound of rain.

"We're almost there, the wheatfields are over that way," Gasparini said.

Then the track joined the road and suddenly Esther saw all the people at work. There was quite a crowd, carts waiting as their horses grazed on the banks of the road, children playing. Near the carts, older men were busy loading the wheat using wooden pitchforks. Most of the fields had already been harvested; women wearing headscarves were leaning over sheaves that they bound together and then pushed out toward the road near the carts. Near them, babies, little tots, were playing with the ears of wheat fallen on the ground. Other children, older ones, were gleaning in the field, stuffing ears into gunnysacks.

The young men were working at the end of the field. Standing a few steps apart from one another, forming a line like infantry soldiers, they moved slowly forward through the wheat, swinging their scythes. That was what Esther had heard from afar when she arrived. With mechanical regularity, the scythes lifted up behind the men, their long blades glinting in the sun, they remained immobile for a moment then suddenly fell back down with a crunching sound into the wheat, and the men made a deep sound with their throats and chests. A hmph! that echoed through the valley.

Esther hid behind the carts because she didn't want anyone to see her, but Gasparini pulled her by the hand and forced her to walk right down the middle of the field. The stubble was sharp and stiff, it pierced through their rope-soled espadrilles, scratched their ankles. The most striking thing was the smell, a smell Esther wasn't familiar with, and maybe it was because of the smell that she'd been frightened when she first arrived. A bitter smell of dust and sweat, a smell that was a mixture of humans and plants. The sun was blinding, it burned your eyelids, your face, your hands. All around them in the field there were women and children in worn clothing whom Esther had never seen before. With a sort of fervent haste, they were gathering up the ears that had fallen from the sheaves and putting them into their gunnysacks. "They're Italians," Gasparini said with a hint of condescension in his voice. "There's no wheat in their country, so they come and glean here." Esther watched the young women in rags intently, their faces half-hidden by faded headscarves. "Where do they come from?" Gasparini pointed to the mountains at the far end of the valley. "They come from Valdieri, from Santa Anna (he said Santanna), they come on foot through the mountains because they're hungry in their country." Esther was surprised, she'd never dreamt that Italians could look like these women and children. But Gasparini was pulling her over toward the line of harvesters. "Look, he's my cousin." A young man in an undershirt, face and arms reddened from the sun, had stopped swinging his scythe. "So, are you going to introduce me to your fiancée?" He burst out laughing, and the other men also stopped to stare at them. Gasparini shrugged his shoulders. With Esther, he walked over to the far end of the field to sit down on an embankment. From there all they could hear was the whooshing of the scythes in the wheat and the deep grunting of the men: hmph! hmph! Gasparini said, "My father says that the Italians are going to lose the war because they have nothing to eat in their country." Esther

replied, "Then maybe they'll come to live here?" Gasparini
answered unhesitatingly, "We wouldn't let them. We'd throw
them out. Besides, the English and the Americans are going
to win the war. My father says that the Germans and the
Italians will soon be defeated." Then, he lowered his voice a
little, "My father is in the Maquis, what about yours?" Esther
thought it over. She wasn't really sure she should answer.
Then she said the same thing, "Mine too, he's in the Maquis."
Gasparini asked, "What does he do?" Esther said, "He helps
Jews get across the mountains, he helps them hide."
Gasparini seemed a little irritated, "That's not the same.
That's not what helping the Maquis is about." Esther already
regretted having talked about all of that. Her mother and
father had told her that she should never talk about the war,
or about the people who came to their house, to anyone. They
had told her that the Italian soldiers gave people money to
turn others in. Maybe Gasparini was going to repeat
everything to Captain Mondoloni? They both remained
silent for a long time, nibbling on the grains of wheat that
they picked one by one from their transparent hulls. Finally,
he said, "What does your father do? I mean what did he do
before the war?" Esther answered, "He was a teacher."
Gasparini seemed interested, "What did he teach?" Esther
said, "He taught history in high school. History and
geography." Gasparini didn't say anything else. He stared
straight out in front of himself, his face was closed. Esther
thought about the way, a little while ago, he had said, "They
don't have anything to eat in their country." A little later,
Gasparini said, "My father has a rifle, he still has it, it's
hidden at our place, in the barn. If you like, I can show it to
you one day." He and Esther again sat there for a while
without saying anything, listening to the sound of the scythes
and the grunting men. The sun hung very still in the center

of the sky, there were no shadows on the ground. Between the spikes of stubble, huge black ants scurried forward, stopped, struck out again. They too were searching for grains of wheat fallen from the sheaves.

"Is it true you're a Jew?" Gasparini asked. Esther looked at him as if she didn't understand. "Tell me, is it true?" the boy repeated. Suddenly there was such an anxious look on his face that Esther answered very rapidly, angrily, "Me? No, no!" Gasparini's face hadn't relaxed. Now he said, "My father says that if the Germans come here, they'll kill all the Jews." Suddenly Esther felt her heart beating faster, painfully, the blood swelled in the veins in her neck, beat in her temples and in her ears. She didn't understand why, but her eyes were full of tears. It was because she'd lied, that was it. She heard the slow, insistent voice of the boy, and her own voice echoing, repeating, "Me? No, no!" Fear, or pain was spilling from her eyes. Up above the fields the sky was almost blackish blue, the light shone on the scythes, on the rocks in the mountains. The sun was scorching her back and shoulders through her dress. Out in the middle of the field, like tireless ants, the women and children in rags continued searching hungrily through the stubble, and their fingers were cut and bloody.

All of a sudden, without saying a word, Esther stood up and left, walking at first, with the spikes of the stubble poking through her espadrilles. Behind her, the slightly hoarse voice of the boy was shouting, "Hélène! Hélène, wait for me! Where are you going?" When she got to the road, where the carts were awaiting their loads of sheaves, she started running as fast as she could toward the village. She was running without looking back, without losing a second, imagining there was a mad dog at her heels so that she could run even faster. The cool air of the valley slipped over her;

after the heat of the wheat fields it felt like water.

She ran till she got a pain in her side and couldn't breathe anymore. Then she sat on the edge of the road, and the silence was terrifying. A truck came along surrounded by a cloud of blue smoke, driven by two carabinieri. The Italians had her climb up in the back and a few minutes later, Esther got off in the town square. She didn't tell her mother what had happened down there where the people were harvesting. The bitter taste of the grains of wheat stayed in her mouth for a long time.

The Italians ended up carting off Mr. Ferne's piano early one morning, in the rain. The news spread quickly, no one knew how. All the children in the town were there, and some old women in aprons too, and Jews wearing their winter caftans, because of the rain. Then the massive, magical piano, all shiny-black with copper candlesticks in the shape of devils, started moving up the street, carried by four Italian soldiers in uniform. Esther watched the strange troop file past, the piano teetering and tottering like a huge coffin, and the black plumes on the soldiers hats bouncing with each step. Several times the soldiers had to stop to catch their breath, and every time they set the piano down on the pavement the cords hummed with a long vibration that sounded like a lament.

That was the day when Esther talked to Rachel for the first time. She followed the cortège from a distance, and then she picked out the shape of Mr. Ferne who was also walking up the street in the rain. Esther hid in the recess of a doorway, to wait, and Rachel stopped right next to her. Drops of water wet Rachel's beautiful red hair, ran down onto her face like tears. Maybe that was why Esther had wanted to become her friend. But the piano had already disappeared at the top of the street, near the Terminus Hotel. Mr. Ferne walked past the girls without seeing them, there was a peculiar grimace on his white face, because of worry, or maybe because of the rain. His thin little gray beard was quivering, as if he were talking to himself, maybe he was cursing the Italian soldiers in his own language. It was comical and sad at the same time, and Esther felt a lump in her throat, because she suddenly understood what war was all about. When there was a war, men, police, and soldiers with strange plumed hats could just come and brazenly take Mr. Ferne's piano from his house and carry it into the dining room of the Terminus Hotel. They could do that even though Mr. Ferne loved his piano more than anything in the world and it was the only thing that mattered to him in life.

Then Rachel walked up the street toward the town square and Esther walked beside her. When they reached the square, they took shelter under a plane tree and watched the rain coming down. When Rachel spoke, a little cloud of steam formed around her lips. Esther was happy to be there, in spite of Mr. Ferne's piano, because she'd wanted to talk to Rachel for a long time but had never dared to. Esther loved her long red hair that fell loosely down onto her shoulders. It shocked a lot of the townspeople, the peasant women and also the religious Jews, that Rachel didn't go to the ceremonies anymore, and that she often talked with the Italian carabinieri in front of the hotel. But she was so beautiful that Esther thought it didn't matter that she wasn't like the others. Esther had often followed Rachel without her knowing—through the streets of the village when she went shopping or when she went for an afternoon stroll in the square with her mother and father. People said a lot of things about her, the boys said she went out at night, in spite of the curfew, and that she went swimming nude in the river. The girls told less extraordinary, but more spiteful stories.

They said that Rachel was dating Captain Mondoloni, that she went to see him at the Terminus Hotel and that they went out on the road together in the armored car. When the war was over and when the Italians were defeated, they would cut off her beautiful hair and put her in front of a firing squad, like all the members of the Gestapo and the Italian army. Esther knew perfectly well they said all of that because they were jealous.

On that day Esther and Rachel stayed together for a long time, talking and watching the rain riddling the surface of the puddles. When it stopped raining, people came out into the square as they did every morning, peasant women in aprons and headscarves, and old men wearing hats and long black caftans. Children started running around too, most of them barefoot and in rags.

Then Rachel pointed to Mr. Ferne. He too was in the square, hiding on the other side of the fountain. He was looking over in the direction of the hotel, as if he would be able to get a glimpse of his piano. There was something both ridiculous and pitiful about his thin shape slipping from tree to tree, craning his neck to try and see inside the hotel while the carabinieri stood smoking by the door, something that made Esther feel ashamed. All of a sudden, she had stood it long enough. She took Rachel's hand and dragged her over to the street with the stream, and they went all the way down to the road above the river. They walked together along the road, still shiny with rain, without saying anything until they reached the bridge. Underneath, the two torrents met, forming whirlpools. A path led to a narrow shingle beach by the converging waters. The sound of the torrents was deafening but Esther thought it was really fine. In that place, nothing else existed in the world, and you couldn't talk to one another. The clouds had parted, the sun shone down on the stones, made the whitewater sparkle.

Esther and Rachel sat on the wet stones for a long time, watching the eddying waters. Rachel pulled out some cigarettes, a strange packet, marked in English. She started smoking and the sweet acrid smoke of the cigarette twirled around her and attracted wasps. At one point, she passed the cigarette to Esther for her to try it, but the smoke made her cough, and Rachel started laughing.

Afterward, they climbed back up the bank because they were cold, and they sat on a low wall in the sunshine. Rachel started talking about her parents in a funny voice—hard, almost cruel. She didn't love them because they were always afraid, and because they'd fled their home in Poland and gone into hiding in France. She didn't talk about the Italians, or about Mondoloni, but all of a sudden she started digging in the pocket of her dress and held out a ring in her open palm.

"Look, someone gave this to me."

It was a very beautiful antique ring, with a dark blue stone that shone out amid other smaller, very white stones.

"It's a sapphire," Rachel said. "And the little ones around it are diamonds."

Esther had never seen anything like it.

"Is it pretty?"

"Yes," said Esther. But she didn't like that dark stone. It had a strange glint that was a little frightening. Esther thought that it was like the war, like the piano that the carabinieri had taken from Mr. Ferne's house. She didn't say anything, but Rachel understood and she immediately put the ring back in her pocket.

"What will you do when the war is over?" Rachel asked. And before Esther had time to think about it, she continued,

"I know what I would like to do. I would like to make music like Mr. Ferne, play the piano, sing. Go to the big cities, to Vienna, Paris, Berlin, to America, everywhere."

She lit up another cigarette, and while she talked about all of that, Esther watched her profile, haloed in her luminous red hair, she watched her arms, her fingers with their long nails. Maybe because of the smoke from the cigarette, because of the sunlight, Esther felt herself getting a bit dizzy. Rachel spoke of the nightlife in Paris, in Warsaw, in Rome, as if she'd really experienced all of that. When Esther talked about Mr. Ferne's music, Rachel suddenly got angry. She said he was an old fool, a bum, with his piano in his kitchen. Esther didn't argue, trying not to destroy the image of Rachel, her delicate profile with its halo of red hair, wanting simply to remain by her side as long as possible and smell the fragrance of her cigarette. But it was sad to hear her talk like that, and think about Mr. Ferne's piano all alone in the vast smoke-filled room at the Terminus Hotel where the carabinieri were drinking and playing cards. It made her think of war, of death, of the image that was forever popping into her mind: that of her father walking through the vast grassy fields, far from the village, disappearing, as if he would never come back.

When Rachel had finished her English cigarette, she threw the stub down into the valley and stood up, brushing off the back of her dress with her hands. Together, not saying a word, they went back toward the village where the chimneys were smoking for the noon meal.

It was already August. Every evening of late, the sky filled with huge white or gray clouds that piled up in fantastic shapes. For several days Esther's father had been leaving early in the morning, wearing his gray flannel suit, carrying a child's school satchel, the same one he used to carry when he went to teach history and geography at the high school in Nice. Esther watched his tense dark face anxiously. He opened the door to the apartment, down below the level of the still-dark narrow street, and he turned around to kiss his daughter. One day Esther asked him, "Where are you going?" He answered almost harshly, "I'm going to see some people." Then he added, "Don't ask me questions, Estrellita. You mustn't speak about any of this, ever, do you understand?" Esther knew that he was going to help the Jews cross the mountains, but she didn't ask anything more. That's why the summer seemed terrifying, despite the beauty of the blue sky, despite the fields with grasses grown so high, despite the song of crickets and the sound of the water rushing over the stones in the torrents. Esther couldn't sit still for a minute in the apartment. On her mother's face she saw her own worry, the silence, the burden of waiting. So, as soon as she drank her morning bowl of hot milk, she opened the door of the apartment and climbed the stairs to the street. She was outside when she heard her mother's voice saying, "Hélène? Are you going out already?" Her mother never called her Esther when someone outside might hear. One evening, as she lay in her bed in the dark room, Esther heard her mother complaining that she spent all her time roaming around, and her father simply responded, "Let her be, these might be her last days..." Ever since then, those words had stuck in her mind: her last days...That was what lured her so irresistibly out of doors. That was what made the sky so blue, the sun so bright, the mountains and the grassy field so fascinating, so all-consuming. At the crack of dawn, Esther started watching the light through the chinks in the cardboard that blocked off the small ventilator window, she waited for the brief cries of birds to call to her, the twittering of sparrows, the shrill whistle of swifts inviting her to come outside. When she could finally open the door and go out into the fresh air in the street, with the icy stream running down the middle of the cobblestones, she had an extraordinary sensation of freedom, a feeling of limitless bliss. She could walk down to the last houses in the village, look out over the whole stretch of the valley—still immense in the morning mist—and her father's words would fade away. Then she'd start running through the big grassy field above the river, without even thinking of vipers, and she'd reach the place where the path led up toward the high mountains. That's where her father went every morning, up into the unknown. Eyes blinded with the morning light, she tried to glimpse the highest peaks, the forest of larches, the gorges, the treacherous ravines. Below, on the floor of the valley, she could hear the voices of children in the river. They were busy catching crayfish, wading into the water up to their thighs, feet sunk deep in the sandy bottoms of the torrent's pools. Esther could distinctly hear the girls laughing, their sharp calls, "Maryse! Maryse!..." She kept walking through the field until the voices and laughter grew faint, disappeared. On the other side of the valley rose the dark slope of the mountain, the screes of red-colored rocks scattered with small thorn bushes. In the grassy field, the sun was already burning hot and Esther felt sweat running down her face, under her arms. Farther up, in the shelter of a few boulders, there was no wind, not a breath, not a sound. That was what Esther came here for, that silence. When there was not a human sound to be heard, only the shrill whirring of insects, and the brief cry of a skylark from time to time, and the rustling grasses, Esther felt so fine. She listened to her heart beating with slow heavy thumps, she even listened to the sound of the air coming out of her nostrils. She didn't understand why she desired that silence. It was just simply right, it was necessary. And so, little by little, the fear dissipated. The sunlight, the sky in which all the clouds were just beginning to swell, and the vast grassy fields where the flies and the bees hung suspended in the light, the somber walls of the mountains and the forests, all of that would go on and on. It wasn't the last day yet, she knew that then, all of it could still remain there, keep going, no one would stop it.

One day Esther wanted to show that place, that secret, to someone. She led Gasparini through the tall grasses all the way up to the boulders. Luckily, Gasparini hadn't mentioned vipers, maybe just to show that he wasn't afraid. But as they neared the screes, Gasparini had said very quickly, "This isn't a good place, I'm going back down." And he turned and ran away. Esther wasn't angry. She was merely surprised that she understood why the boy had run off so rapidly. He didn't need to know that everything would last, that everything had to keep going day after day, for years and centuries, and that no one could stop it.

It wasn't the fields full of viper grass that Esther was afraid of. What frightened her was the harvest. The fields of wheat were like trees shedding their leaves. Esther went back to see the harvest once again, back to the place she'd gone with Gasparini, way down in the valley, near Roquebillière.

This time the wheat was almost entirely cut. The line of men armed with their long glittering blades had broken up, there were only a few isolated groups. They were cutting the wheat higher up in the fields, in narrow terraces on the flanks of the mountain. The children were binding the last sheaves. The poor women and children were wandering through the stubble but their sacks remained empty.

Esther sat on the embankment looking out on the bare fields. She didn't understand why she felt so sad, so angry,

with such a blue sky and the sun beating down on the
stubbled fields. Gasparini came and sat down beside her.
They didn't say anything. They watched the harvesters
moving along the terraces. Gasparini was holding a fistful
of ears and they crunched on the grains of wheat, slowly
savoring the bittersweet taste. Now Gasparini never spoke
of the war anymore, or of Jews. He seemed tense and
worried. He was a boy of fifteen or sixteen, but already
broad and strong as a man, with cheeks that flushed easily
like a girl's. Esther felt very different from him, but she quite
liked him anyway. When his friends walked by on the road
they jeered him and he looked at them angrily, got halfway
up as if he were going to fight them.

One day Gasparini came to get Esther at her house, early in
the morning. He came down the little stairway from the road
and knocked at the door. Esther's mother opened the door.
She looked at him for a moment, not understanding, then
she recognized him and asked him to come into the kitchen.
It was the first time he'd been to Esther's house. He looked
around—the dark narrow room, the wooden table with
benches, the cast-iron stove, the pots sitting balanced on a
board. When Esther came in she almost burst out laughing
seeing him looking so sheepish standing in front of the table,
his eyes trained on the waxed tablecloth. From time to time,
he shooed a fly away with the back of his hand.

Elizabeth brought out a bottle of cherry juice that she'd
made in the spring. Gasparini drank the glass of juice, then
he took a handkerchief from his pocket to wipe his mouth.
The silence in the kitchen made everything seem to last
much longer. Finally he decided to talk, in a slightly gruff
voice. "I wanted to ask permission to take Hélène to church
on Friday, for the celebration." He looked at Esther standing

there in front of him as if she could help him. "What celebration?" asked Elizabeth. "Friday is the celebration of the Madonna," explained Gasparini. "The Madonna should return to the mountains, she'll be leaving the church." Elizabeth turned to her daughter, "Well? I suppose it's up to you to decide?" Esther said soberly, "If my parents consent, I'll go." Elizabeth said, "You have my permission, but you'll have to ask your father too."

The ceremony took place on Friday, as planned. The carabinieri issued an authorization and first thing in the morning people started gathering in the little village square in front of the church. Inside the church, children had lit candles and hung bouquets of flowers. There were mostly old men and women because many of the younger men were prisoners and hadn't come back from the war. But the teenage girls came wearing their low-necked summer dresses, barelegged, with espadrilles on their feet and only a shawl over their hair. Gasparini came to pick up Esther. He was wearing a light gray suit with knickers that belonged to his older brother who had worn them only once, on the day of his Solemn Communion. For the first time in his life, he had put on a tie, it was burgundy-colored. Esther's mother smiled a little mockingly at the young peasant dressed in his Sunday best, but Esther shot a reproachful glance at her. Esther's father shook Gasparini's hand and said a few friendly words. Gasparini was very impressed with the tall figure Esther's father cut and also because he was a teacher. When Esther had asked her father's permission, he'd said without hesitating, "Yes, it's important for you to go to this celebration." He'd said that so seriously that it intrigued Esther.

Now, seeing the church filled with people, she understood why it was so important. The crowd had come from all over, even from isolated farms up in the mountains, from the sheepfolds of the Boréon, or Mollières. In the open square in front of the Terminus Hotel with the Italian flag flying from its roof, the carabinieri and soldiers watched the throngs go by.

Around ten o'clock the ceremony began. The priest entered the chapel, followed by part of the crowd. In its midst were three men dressed in dark blue suits. Gasparini whispered in Esther's ear, "Look, that's my cousin." Esther recognized the young man who had been harvesting the wheat near Roquebillière. "When the war is over, he'll be the one who will carry the Madonna into the mountains." The church was packed and there was not enough room for the children. They waited on the porch in front of the church in the sun. When the bell started ringing, a ripple went through the crowd and the three men appeared, carrying the statue. It was the first time Esther had seen the statue of the Madonna. It represented a small woman with a waxen face, holding in her arms a baby with a strangely adult look in his eyes. The statue was draped in a large cloak of blue satin that shone in the sunlight. Its hair also shone, it was black and as thick as a horse's mane. People moved aside to make way for the statue that rocked back and forth over the heads of the crowd, and the three men went back inside the church. From the hubbub, rose the first notes of Ave Maria. "When the war is over, my cousin will go with the others, they'll take the statue up to the sanctuary in the mountains," repeated Gasparini rather impatiently. When the ceremony was finished, everyone flooded out into the square. Esther stood on her tiptoes to try and get a glimpse of the Italian soldiers. Their gray uniforms stood out starkly in the shade of the lime trees. But it was really Rachel that Esther wanted to see.

A little off to one side, the old Jews were watching too. You could pick them out in the distance because of their black clothing, their hats, the scarves on the women's heads, their pallid faces. Despite the hot sporadic bursts of sun, they kept their caftans on. They stood there looking on without speaking to one another, stroking their beards. The Jewish children didn't mingle with the well-dressed crowd. They stood very still next to their parents.

All of a sudden, Esther saw Tristan. He was standing on the edge of the square with the Jewish children. He wasn't moving, just standing there staring. He had a funny expression on his face, a grimace against the bright sunlight.

Esther felt the blood rushing under her skin. She pulled away from Gasparini's hand and marched straight over to Tristan. Her heart was pounding heavily, she thought it was anger. "Why are you always watching me? Why do you spy on me?" He stepped back a little. His deep blue eyes shone, but he didn't respond. "Go away! Find something else to do, leave me alone, you're not my brother!" Esther heard Gasparini's voice calling her, "Hélène! Come back, where are you going?" There was such an anxious look in Tristan's eyes that she stopped for a moment and her voice grew softer, she said to him, "I'll be back, I'm sorry, I don't know why I said that to you." She pushed through the crowd with her head down, without answering Gasparini. The girls stepped aside to let her by. She started walking down the street with the stream; it was deserted. But she didn't want to go back home, she didn't want to have to answer her mother's questions. Once far from the square, she heard the sound of human voices swelling, laughter, calls, and over it all, a sort of humming, the voice of the priest chanting in the church, *Ave, Ave, Ave Maria...*

As the afternoon drew to a close, Esther went back to the square. Most of the people were gone, but there was a group of boys and girls over by the lime trees. When she walked up to them, Esther heard the sound of accordion music. In the center of the square, by the fountain, women were dancing with each other, or else with very young boys who came up only to their shoulders. The Italian soldiers were standing in front of the hotel, smoking and listening to the music.

Now Esther was looking for Rachel. Slowly, she walked over toward the hotel, her heart racing. She glanced over in the direction of the main room, and through the open door she saw the soldiers and the carabinieri. On Mr. Ferne's piano a gramophone was playing a slow, nasal-sounding mazurka. Outside, the women spun around, their red faces shining in the sunlight. Esther walked past them, past the boys, past the carabinieri—she walked up to the door of the hotel. The sun was very low in the sky; it barely lit the inside of the main room through the windows overlooking the garden. The light was painful for Esther, it made her dizzy. Maybe it was because of what her father had said, that everything had to stop. When Esther went into the room, she felt relieved. But her heart still beat heavily in her chest. She saw Rachel. She was with the plumed soldiers, in the middle of the room in which the tables and chairs had been pushed back against the walls, and she was dancing with Mondoloni. There were other women in the room, but Rachel was the only one dancing. The others were watching her, how she turned and whirled around, with her pale-colored dress flying up and showing her slender legs, how her bare arm lay lightly on the soldier's shoulder. At times, the carabinieri and the soldiers stopped in front of Esther, and she had to stand on her tiptoes to see. Because of the loud music, Esther couldn't hear Rachel's voice, but she thought she heard an exclamation, a burst of laughter from time to time. Never had Rachel seemed so beautiful to her. She must have already had quite a lot to drink, but she was the sort who could hold her liquor well. She simply held herself very straight as she turned and turned to the sound of the mazurka, and her long dark red hair swept lightly across her back. In vain, Esther tried to attract her attention. Her brown face was thrown backward, she was gone, far from that place, in another world, being swept along with the dancing and the sounds of the music. The soldiers and the carabinieri were all turned facing her, watching her as they smoked and drank, and Esther thought she heard them laughing. The children had come up and were standing in front of the door, trying to see in, the women were leaning forward in an attempt to make out the lithe silhouette dancing in the main room. Then the carabinieri turned around, they motioned with their hands, and everyone drew back. Outside in the square, the young people kept their distance, on the other side of the fountain. None of them seemed to be paying any attention. That's what made Esther's heart beat so fast. She felt that something wasn't right, it was as if there was a lie somewhere. The young people were pretending that they didn't see, but it was Rachel they were thinking of—deep down, they hated her even more than they hated the Italian soldiers.

The music continued, with the nasal voice, the polkas beat out on Mr. Ferne's piano, the strangled voice of the clarinet knotted in the air.

When Esther left the hotel, Gasparini came up and stood in front of her. His eyes glinted with anger. "Come on, we're going for a walk." Esther shook her head. She walked down the narrow street till she came to the place where you can see out over the valley. She wanted to be alone, not hear the music or the voices anymore. At one point, Gasparini grabbed hold of her wrist and pulled her over to him clumsily, holding her by the waist, as if he wanted to dance. His face was red from the heat, the tie was strangling him. He leaned toward Esther, tried to kiss her. His smell filled Esther's nostrils, a heavy smell that frightened and attracted her at the same time, a man-smell. She started pushing him away, saying at first, "Leave me alone, go away!" Then she started struggling fiercely, she scratched him and he just stood in the middle of the street, puzzled. The boys were forming a circle around them, laughing. Then Tristan jumped on Gasparini, grabbing him around the neck, he was trying to get a good hold on him, but he was too light, he was left hanging there, his feet dangling in the air. With a mere jab of the elbow, Gasparini threw him off and sent him rolling on the ground. He shouted, "You little snot, try that again and I'll beat your head in!" Esther started running through the streets as fast as she could, then she headed down through the fields to the torrent. She stopped running, listened to her heart thudding in her chest, in her throat. Even there near the river she could still hear the sad, whining music of the party, the clarinet endlessly repeating the same phrase on the record while Rachel swung around the room with Mondoloni, her pale face impervious and distant like that of a blind woman.

Nights were very dark, because of the curfew. You had to draw the curtains at the windows, plug up all the cracks with rags and cardboard. Sometimes the men from the Maquis came in the afternoon. They sat down on the benches around the table covered with a waxed cloth in the narrow kitchen. Esther knew them well, but she didn't know most of their names. Some came from the village or nearby, they left before nightfall. Some came from far away, from Nice or Cannes, sent by Ignace Finck, Gutman, Wister, Appel. Some even came from the Italian Maquis. Among them, there was one whom Esther liked very much. He was a lad with hair as red as Rachel's, and his name was Mario. He came from beyond the mountains, where the Italian peasants and shepherds were fighting against the fascists. Whenever he came, he was always so tired that he stayed overnight, sleeping on some cushions on the kitchen floor. He didn't talk much with the other maquisards. He spent his time with Esther instead. He told her funny stories, half in French, half in Italian, punctuated with great bursts of laughter. He had small eyes that were surprisingly green, snake eyes, thought Esther. Sometimes when he'd spent the night in the kitchen, he took Esther for a walk around the village at dawn, without even worrying about the soldiers in the Terminus Hotel.

She went with him out into the fields, up above the river. Together they walked through the tall grass, him in front, her following in the path he made in the grass. He was the one who mentioned vipers first. But he wasn't afraid of them. He said that he could tame them, and even catch them, by whistling at them like dogs.

One morning he took Esther out even farther into the fields, beyond the place where the two streams met. Esther was walking behind him, her heart racing wildly, listening to Mario who was making odd whistling sounds—soft and shrill—a sort of music she'd never heard before. The heat of the sun was already swirling thickly in the grasses, and the mountains around the valley looked like giant walls from which the clouds sprang into being. They walked for a long time through the tall grass with Mario's soft whistling sounds that seemed to come from all sides at once, they gave you a slightly dizzy feeling. Suddenly Mario stopped, holding his hand up in the air. Esther slipped noiselessly up against his back. Mario turned toward her. His green eyes shone. In a whisper he said, "Look!" Through the grass, Esther saw something she wasn't quite sure of lying on the shingle beach by the riverbank. It looked like a thick rope made of two short twisted fibers—the color of dead leaves— that shone in the light as if someone had just taken it out of the water. Suddenly Esther shuddered—the rope was moving! Horrified, Esther watched through the grass as the two intertwined vipers slithered and twisted over the beach. At one point their heads parted, two short snouts, eyes with vertical pupils, mouths open. The vipers remained stuck together, staring fixedly at each other, as if in ecstasy. Then their bodies started twisting on the rocks again, slithering between the pebbles, coiling to one side. Clinging to one another in knots that slipped up and down, came undone, lashing their tails like whips. They continued to slide, roll, and, despite the crashing of the river, Esther thought she heard the scraping sound of scales running over one another. "Are they fighting?" Esther asked, trying her best to speak softly. Mario was watching the snakes. The whole of his thick face was concentrated in his gaze, his two narrowly slit eyes like those of the snakes. He turned toward Esther and said, "No, they're making love." Then Esther watched even more intently as the two entangled vipers slithered over the beach, through the pebbles, without noticing their presence. It lasted a very long time, the snakes remaining motionless and cold at times like bits of branch, then suddenly quivering and whipping the ground, so closely joined that you couldn't see their heads anymore. In the end, their bodies relaxed and their heads dropped to the ground, each to one side. Esther could see the frozen pupil, like a treacherous loophole, and their bodies puffed up with their breathing and the light shining on their scales. Very slowly, one of the vipers loosened the knot, it slipped away and disappeared in the grass by the river. When the other began moving away, Mario started whistling in his strange way, between his teeth, almost without opening his lips, a tenuous whistling—soft, almost inaudible. The snake lifted its head and stared straight at Mario and Esther standing there in the grass. Under that gaze, Esther felt her heart dip and waver. The viper hesitated a moment, its wide head making a right angle to its upright body. Then, in the wink of an eye, it too disappeared across the grassy field.

Mario and Esther went back toward the village. They didn't say anything the whole way, walking through the tall grass, simply being careful about where they put their feet. When they got to the road, Esther asked, "You never kill them?" Mario started laughing. "Yes, yes, I know how to kill them too." He picked up a small stick on the edge of the road and showed her how to do it, giving a sharp rap on the snake's neck, near the head. Esther asked again, "And could you have killed them today?" A strange look came over Mario's face. He shook his head. "No, today I couldn't have. It would have been wrong to kill them."

That was why Esther liked Mario so much. One day, instead of telling her stories, he had told her a little about his life, just a few snatches. Before the war he had been a shepherd, over by Valdieri. He hadn't wanted to go to war, he had hidden in the mountains. But the fascists killed all his sheep and his dog, and Mario had joined the Maquis.

Now Esther had phony papers. One afternoon, some men came with Mario into the kitchen and they put ID cards down on the table for everyone, for Esther, for her mother and father, for Mario too. Esther looked at the bit of yellow cardboard with her father's photo on it for a long time. Written there she saw:

Name: JAUFFERT. First name: Pierre. Middle name: Michel

Date of birth: April 10, 1910. Place of birth: Marseille (Bouches-du-Rhône).

Profession: Salesman

Features:

Nose:

Bridge: straight

Base: medium

Size: medium

General shape of face: long

Complexion: fair

Eyes: green

Hair: light brown

Then her mother's card, Name: JAUFFERT, Maiden name:

Leroy, First name: Madeleine, born February 3, 1912 in Pontivy (Morbihan), No profession. And her own, JAUFFERT Hélène, born February 22, 1931, in Nice (Alpes-Maritimes), no profession. Features: Nose: Bridge: straight, Base: medium, Size: medium, General shape of face: oval, Complexion: fair, Eyes: green, Hair: black.

The men talked for a long time sitting around the table, their faces lit fantastically by the oil lamp. Esther tried to listen to what they were saying, without understanding, as if they were train robbers planning a job. She watched Mario's broad face, his red hair, his narrow, slanting eyes, and she thought that maybe he was dreaming about the vipers in the grassy fields, or about the hares that he caught in his traps on full-moon nights.

When the men spoke with her father, there was always a name that she couldn't forget because it sounded so fine, like the name of a hero in one of her father's history books: Angelo Donati. Angelo Donati said this, did that, and the men all nodded in agreement. Angelo Donati had a boat ready in Livorno, a big motorized sailboat that would take all the fugitives aboard and save them. The boat would cross the sea and take the Jews to Jerusalem, far from the Germans. Esther listened to that, lying on the floor on the cushions that Mario used for a bed and she fell half way asleep, dreaming of Angelo Donati's boat, of the long journey across the sea to Jerusalem. Then Elizabeth got up, she wrapped her arms around Esther and together they walked to the little alcove room where Esther's bed was. Before going to sleep, Esther asked, "Tell me, when will we go away on Angelo Donati's boat? When will we go to Jerusalem?" Esther's mother kissed her, told her jokingly, but in a low voice, her throat tightening with worry, "Go to sleep now, never speak of Angelo Donati to anyone, do you understand? It's a secret." Esther said, "But is it true that the boat will take everyone to Jerusalem?" Elizabeth answered, "It's true, and we'll go too, maybe, we'll go to Jerusalem." Esther kept her eyes wide open in the darkness, she listened to the sound of the voices echoing softly in the little kitchen, Mario's laughter. Then there were footsteps outside dying away, the door closed. When her mother and father lay down in the big bed next to hers and she could hear them breathing, she went to sleep.

It was already the end of summer, with rain every afternoon and the sound of water streaming down over the roof and through all the gutters. In the morning the sun shone brightly over the mountains and Esther would hardly take time to swallow her bowl of milk to get outdoors more quickly. She waited for Tristan in the square by the fountain and then they and the other children ran down the street with the stream all the way to the river. The rains had barely troubled the crashing, cold waters of the Boréon. The boys waited down at the bottom and Esther went up with the other girls to the place where the torrent cascaded down between two blocks of rock. They undressed in the bushes. Like most of the girls, Esther bathed in her panties, but there were some, like Judith, who were too shy to take off their slips. The greatest part was getting into the water, hanging on to the rocks, right where the current was strongest, and letting the water run over your body. The smooth water poured down, pushing against your shoulders and chest, sliding over your hips and along your legs making its unbroken sound. Then you could forget everything, the cold water cleansed you to the very core, washed away everything that was bothering you, burning within you. Judith, Esther's friend (she wasn't really her friend, not like Rachel was, but they sat together in Mr. Seligman's class), had talked about baptism absolving sins. Esther thought that this is what it must feel like, a smooth, cold river flowing over you and cleansing you. When Esther came out of the torrent into the sunlight and stood unsteadily on the flat rock, she felt as if she were brand new and as if all the bad feelings and all the anger had disappeared. Afterward, the girls went back down to where the boys were waiting. They'd been scavenging around in vain in the holes of the torrent looking for crayfish, and, to get even for not having caught anything, they splashed water at the girls.

So then everyone sat down on a large flat rock above the torrent and waited, watching the water. The sun climbed in the still-cloudless sky. Light filtered into the forest of birch and chestnut trees. Irritated wasps flew about, drawn by the drops of water caught in their hair, on their bare skin. Esther was very attentive to every detail, every shadow, she watched with an almost pained scrutiny everything near and far: the line of Caïres' ridge against the sky, the pines bristling on the hilltops, the prickly grasses, the stones, the gnats hanging suspended in the light. The shouts of children, the laughter of girls, each word echoed strangely in her ears, two or three times, like the barking of dogs. They were unrecognizable, incomprehensible, Gasparini, with his red face, his short-cropped hair, his broad man-shoulders, and the others, Maryse, Anne, Bernard, Judith, all so thin in their wet clothing, their eyes hidden in the shadows of their brows, their silhouettes, both frail and distant at the same time. But Tristan wasn't like the others. He was so awkward, he had such gentle eyes. Of late, whenever they went for a walk around the village, Esther would hold his hand. They were playing at being in love. They went down to the torrent and she would lure him into the gorge, jumping from rock to rock. She thought that was the thing she was best at in life: running through the rocks, leaping lightly, calculating her stride, choosing which route to take in a quarter of a second. Tristan tried to follow, but Esther was too fast for him. She bounded along so quickly that no one could have followed her. She jumped without thinking, barefoot, holding her espadrilles, then she would stop, listening for the panting breath of the boy who wasn't able to keep up with her. When she'd gone quite a ways up the torrent, she stopped by the water's edge, hidden by a mass of rock, listening acutely to all the sounds—cracking things, insects whirring—mingling with the crashing flow of water. She could hear dogs barking far off in the distance and then, Tristan's voice calling her name "Hélène! Hé-lè-ne!" She enjoyed not answering, staying there huddled up in the shelter of the rock, because it was as if she were in charge of her life, as if she could decide everything that would ever happen to her. It was a game, but she didn't tell anyone about it. Who would have understood? When Tristan had grown hoarse from calling, he followed the torrent back down and Esther came out of her hiding place. She climbed the steep slope up to the path, went over to the cemetery. From there, she would wave her arms and shout so that Tristan would see her. But sometimes she went back down to the village alone, walked home, threw herself on her bed with her face buried in the pillow, and cried. She didn't know what about.

It was the end, the most scorching part of the summer, when the grass fields turned yellow and straw stalks fermented at the edge of the fields with pungent warmth. Esther had never been out that far alone, past the place where the shepherds kept their flocks in winter—windowless drystone huts, vaulted cellars like caves. Suddenly the clouds appeared, cutting off the light as if a giant hand had opened up in the sky. Esther had gone so far she thought she was lost, just like in her dreams, when her father would disappear in the field of tall grass. It wasn't really all that terrifying, feeling as if you were lost at the mouth of the gorges, deep in the dark mountains. It made you shudder a bit on account of the wolf stories. Mario had told her about the wolves in Italy, they walked through the winter snow in single file, went down into the valleys to carry off lambs and young goats. But maybe Esther had shuddered because of the sharp wind bearing the rain along in its path. Standing up on a rock above the bushes, she could see the gray clouds covering the flanks of the mountains, making their way up the narrow valley. The sweeping curtain was engulfing rocky cliffs, forests, great boulders. The wind began to blow harder, bitterly cold after the warmth of the fermenting straw. Esther started running, trying to make it back to the shepherds' huts before the rain. But the icy drops were already spattering heavily on the ground. Life was taking its revenge, catching up on the time Esther had stolen in her hiding places. She was running, her heart leaping wildly in her chest.

The sheepfold was immense, like a cave. It formed a long tunnel penetrating far back into the mountain. There were bats up in the shadows of the ceiling. Esther huddled in the doorway, half obstructed with a tangle of roots. Now that the rain was falling, Esther felt a little calmer. Flashes of lightning lit up the clouds. Water was beginning to flood down the side of the hill, forming large red streams. Soon Mr. Seligman would reopen school, the days would be getting shorter and shorter and snow would fall in the mountains. Esther thought about that as she watched the rain coming down and the streams rushing past her. She thought something was going to happen, something no one knew about.

Lately, these last few days, people just weren't the same as they used to be. There was something hurried about them, in the way they spoke, in the way they moved. The children had changed most of all. They were impatient, irritable, when they were playing, when they went fishing or swimming in the torrent, even when they were running about in the square. Gasparini had said again, "The Germans will be coming soon, they'll take all the Jews away." He said that as if it were an absolute certainty, and Esther had felt her throat tighten because that was what time was bringing and what she wanted to prevent. She said, "Then they'll take me away too." Gasparini looked at her sharply, "If you have false papers, they won't take you away." He said, "Hélène, that's not a Jewish name." Esther answered immediately, in a calm, cold voice, "My name's not Hélène, my name's Esther. It's a Jewish name." Gasparini said, "If the Germans come, you'll have to hide." He seemed unsure of himself for the first time. He added, "If the German's come, I'll hide you in the barn."

In the square, the boys were talking about Rachel. When Esther came up to them, they jabbed her away with their elbows, "Get lost! You're too little!" But Anne knew what they were talking about because her older brother was in the group. She heard them say that they'd found out where Captain Mondoloni went with Rachel—an old barn on the other side of the bridge down by the river. It was midday, but instead of going to eat lunch, Esther ran down the road all the way to the bridge, then she set out across the fields toward the barn. When she reached it, she heard the cawing of crows in the silent afternoon, and she thought that the boys had made the whole story up. But when she drew nearer to the old barn, she saw them hiding behind the bushes. There were several boys, older ones, and some girls too. The barn was built straddling two terraced embankments, down below the road level. Esther went down the slope without making a sound, over to the barn. Three boys were lying in the grass, and they were peeking into the barn through an opening above the wall, just under the roof. When Esther reached them, they stood up and started beating her, without saying a word. They kicked and punched her while one of them held her arms. Esther was thrashing around, her eyes were filled with tears, but she wasn't crying out loud. She tried to get a neck-lock on the boy who was holding her and he stumbled backwards. The boy backed away with Esther hanging on to his neck with all her might while the others pummeled her on the back to make her let go. Finally she fell to the ground, her eyes blurred with a cloud of blood. The boys climbed back up the embankment and ran off down the road. Then the barn door opened and through the red haze Esther saw Rachel looking at her. She was wearing her pretty pale-colored dress, the sun made her hair shine like copper. Then the captain came out after her, straightening his clothes. He had his revolver in his hand. When he saw Esther on the bank of the road and the boys running off, he burst out laughing and said something in Italian. At the same time, Rachel started screaming, in a strangely shrill and vulgar voice that Esther didn't recognize. She was climbing up the slope of the embankment with her gleaming hair, and she was picking up stones and throwing them awkwardly at the fleeing boys without succeeding in hitting them. Esther was in such pain that she couldn't get to her feet. She started crawling up the bank, desperately seeking some hole to hide in, to block out the shame and the fear. But Rachel came over, sat down in the grass beside her and stroked her hair and face. In a strange voice, hoarse from having screamed, she was saying: "It's nothing, sweetheart, it's all over..." and so they sat there alone in the sunshine on the grassy slope. Esther was trembling with cold and with exhaustion, she was watching the light in Rachel's red hair, smelling the odor of her body. Afterward, they went down to the torrent and Rachel carefully helped her wash her face where the blood had dried. Esther was so tired that she needed to lean on Rachel to walk back up the slope to the village. She wished it would start raining right then and not stop until winter.

That was the evening Esther learned of Mario's death. There had been a faint tapping at the door in the night and Esther's father let some men in, a Jew named Gutman, and two men from Lantosque. Esther got out of bed and cracked open the bedroom door, squinting her eyes in the light from the kitchen. She stood in the doorway watching the men whispering around the table as if they were talking to the oil lamp. Elizabeth was sitting with them, she too was watching the lamp flame, saying nothing. Esther understood right away that something serious had happened. When the three men went out into the night again, Esther's father noticed her standing there at the door in her nightgown, and at first he said to her, almost harshly, "What are you doing there? Go back to bed!" Then he came over and held her closely in his arms, as if he were sorry to have scolded her. Elizabeth came over with tears running from her eyes. She said: "It's Mario, he's dead." Her father explained what had happened. It was only words, and yet for Esther, they were interminable, it was a story that repeated itself over and over again, incessantly, like in your dreams. That afternoon, while Esther was going down the road to the abandoned barn, the place where Rachel went to meet Captain Mondoloni, Mario was walking through the mountains, his knapsack filled with plastic explosives and delayed-action detonators, and dynamite sticks too, on his way to join the group that was going to blow up the power lines to Berthemont, where the Germans had recently set up their headquarters. The sun was shining down on the grass as Esther walked toward the

deserted barn, and at that very same instant, Mario was
walking alone through the fields at the foot of the mountains,
and while he walked, he must certainly have been whistling
gently to the vipers, just as he always did, and he was looking
up at the very same sky that she was, hearing the very same
crows cawing. Mario had hair as red as Rachel's, Rachel
standing in the sunlight with her pale dress unhooked in the
back, her white shoulders glowing in the sun, so alive, so
attractive. Mario liked Rachel a lot, he told Esther so himself
one day and when he'd confided that to her, he blushed—or
more precisely, he turned bright red—and Esther had burst
out laughing because of the color of his cheeks. He told
Esther that when the war was over, he would take Rachel
dancing on Saturdays, and Esther didn't have the heart to
tell him that he wasn't Rachel's type, that she liked Italian
officers, that she went dancing with Captain Mondoloni, and
that people said she was a whore, and that they'd crop off her
hair when the war was over. Mario was taking the sack of
explosives to the men in the Maquis, over Berthemont way,
he was walking quickly through the fields in order to get
there before nightfall because he wanted to get back to spend
the night in Saint-Martin. That was why Esther got up when
the three men knocked at the door, because she thought it
was Mario. Esther was slipping through the dry grass,
toward the ruined barn. In the warm, damp barn Rachel was
lying close against the captain, and he...he was kissing her
on the mouth, down her neck, all over. It was the girls that
said all of that, but they hadn't seen a thing, because it was
much too dark in the barn. Only they'd listened to the sounds,
the sighing, and the rustling of clothing. So when they
finished beating Esther up, the boys fled, ran up to the road,
disappeared, and she was dragging herself through the grass
on the bank with that red cloud before her eyes. And that

was when she had heard the sound of the explosion, far away in the distance, down in the valley. That was why the captain came out of the barn holding his revolver, because he too, had heard the explosion. But Esther hadn't paid much attention to it because just then, at that very same instant, Rachel was standing there in front of the barn with all that red hair shining like a mane, and she was screaming insults at the boys and sitting down next to Esther. And the captain had started laughing and walked off down the road just as Rachel was sitting down in the grass to stroke Esther's hair. There had only been one explosion, such a terrific one that Esther had felt the pressure of the blast in her eardrums. When the men from the Maquis arrived, all they found was a huge crater in the grass, a gaping hole with burnt edges, smelling of powder. Searching through the grass around the hole, they'd also found a clump of red hair, and that's how they knew that Mario was dead. That was all that was left of him. Nothing but a clump of red hair. Now Esther was crying in her father's arms. She could feel the tears come brimming up out of her eyes, go running down her cheeks, along her nose and chin, dribbling off onto her father's shirt. And he was saying things about Mario, about everything he'd done, about his courage, but Esther wasn't really crying about that. She didn't know what she was crying about. Maybe it was on account of all these days that she'd spent running through the grass, in the sunshine, on account of the exhaustion, and also on account of Mr. Ferne's music. Maybe it was because the summer was burning itself out, the harvest, and the straw stalks moldering, the black clouds that gathered every evening, and the rain falling in cold drops, giving birth to red streams that rutted the mountain. She was so very tired, she wanted to go to sleep, forget everything, be somewhere else, be someone else, with another name, a real one, not

The train trip from Paris. The cars were packed, there wasn't a single seat left. Mama lay down on the floor on a piece of cardboard in the aisle in front of the door to the toilet, and I remained standing as long as I could to keep an eye on our suitcases. Our two suitcases are wound about with twine to reinforce them. They hold all of our treasures. Our clothing, our toiletries, our books, our pictures, some souvenirs. Mama brought along two kilos of sugar because she says it will surely be in short supply over there. I don't have many clothes. I brought my white cotton summer dress, a pair of gloves, an extra pair of shoes, and above all the books I love, the books my father used to read us sometimes in the evenings after dinner, *Nicholas Nickleby* and *The Adventures of Mr. Pickwick*. They're my favorites. When I feel like crying, or laughing, or thinking about something else, all I have to do is pick one of them up; I open it at random and I immediately find the passage I need.

As for Mama, she brought only one book. Before Mama left, Uncle Simon Ruben gave her the Book of the Beginning, *Sepher Berasith*, that's what it's called. Mama fell asleep on the dirty floor in the aisle of the car, in spite of the jolting couplings and the door to the toilet that was banging next to her head, and the smell...Every now and again someone who needed to use the toilet came down to the end of the aisle. When they saw Mama sleeping on the floor on the piece of cardboard, they turned around and looked elsewhere. But still, there was one person who tried to go in. He stood in front of Mama and said, "Excuse me!" as if she would wake up immediately and get to her feet. She kept on sleeping, so he shouted several times, louder and louder, "Excuse me! Excuse me! Excuse me!" Then he leaned down to drag her out of the way. I don't know what came over me then, but I just couldn't stand it, no, that cruel fat man who was going to wake Mama up so he could go to the toilet in peace. I jumped on him and started pummeling him with my fists and scratching him, but I didn't say anything, didn't shout, I had my jaws clenched and there were tears in my eyes. He backed off as if a wildcat had pounced on him; he pushed me away and started yelling in a strange, high-pitched voice, filled with anger and fear, "You haven't heard the last of me! Just wait and see!" And he walked off. So then I lay down on the floor too, next to Mama who hadn't even woken up, and I put my arms around her and I slept a little, it was a sleep filled with noises and jerks that made me feel nauseated.

In Marseille, it was raining. We waited for hours on the huge platform. Mama and I weren't the only ones. There were a lot of people on the platforms, crowded together amidst the luggage. We waited all night long. A cold wind was blowing over the platforms, the rain made rings of fog around the electric lights. People were lying on the ground, leaning against their suitcases. Some were wrapped in blankets from the Red Cross. Some children cried a little, then fell suddenly asleep, overcome with fatigue. Some men dressed in black, Jewish men, talked on endlessly in their language. Talking and smoking, sitting on their luggage, and their voices echoed strangely in the hollowness of the station.

When we'd gotten off the train in Marseille, a little before midnight, no one said anything to us, but a rumor went from one person to the next, down the length of the platform: there would be no train for Toulon till three or four o'clock in the morning. Maybe we would have to spend the whole night waiting on the platform, but what difference did it make? Time had ceased to exist for us. We'd been traveling, been out in the open for so long in a world where time no longer existed.

That's when I saw him on the same platform, under the large clock that looked like a waxen moon. He'd been on the platform of the station in Paris before the train left, so long ago that it seemed like weeks had gone by. He was making his way through the crowd just when the train came into the station in a great fury of hissing steam and screeching brakes. He was tall, thin, and his golden hair and beard made him look like a shepherd. I say that, because now I know that's what his name is, Jacques Berger. So that's what I nicknamed him, the Shepherd.

He was walking against the tide of the crowd glancing around, looking for something, someone, a relative, a friend. When he reached the point where he was almost facing me, his eyes locked on mine for such a long time that I had to turn away and I bent down over my suitcase as if I were looking for something so he wouldn't see me blushing.

I'd forgotten about him, not completely forgotten, but the train, the noise of the couplings, the jolts, and Mama who was sleeping like a sick child by the toilet door, all of that kept me from thinking about anyone at all. G__! I so hate traveling! How can anyone take the train or the boat for pleasure! I would like to spend my whole life in one place, just watching the days go by, the clouds, the birds, dreaming. At the other end of the platform—just as in Paris—the Shepherd in question was standing, as if he were waiting for someone, a relative, a friend. Despite the distance I could see his eyes in the shadow of his brow.

Since we might have to wait on that platform all night long, we needed to get organized. I laid the two suitcases down flat and Mama sat down on the ground, leaning the top part of her body against the suitcases. I planned on doing the same soon. When will it all be over? Today I feel as though I haven't stopped traveling since the day I was born, in trains, in buses, on mountain roads, and also moving from one apartment to another, to Nice, to Saint-Martin, to Berthemont. One day Mama said that all those names were cursed, that we shouldn't ever say them again. Not even think about them again.

The Shepherd spoke to me a little earlier when I was coming back from the toilets in the station. I was walking under the clock and there he was, sitting on his suitcase among all the people lying down. Next to him sat the group of Jewish men dressed in black, talking and smoking. He said, "Hello, Miss," in his rather deep voice. He said, "It's quite a long wait here on this train platform," and, "You aren't feeling too cold, are you?" with a Parisian accent, I think. I noticed he had a little scar next to his lip; I thought of my father. I don't remember what I said, maybe I walked away without answering, with my head down, because I was so tired, so desperately sleepy. I think I grunted something unpleasant so I could get away faster, settle down with my torso leaning against the suitcase, my legs curled up sideways, as close to Mama as possible. I don't think it had ever occurred to me before that she could die.

Nights are long when it's cold and you're waiting for a train. I wasn't able to sleep a single minute, despite the fatigue, despite the emptiness all around me. I kept looking around, as if to make sure that nothing had changed, that everything was still real. I looked at it all, the immense station with its glass dome with the rain streaming down, the platforms stretching away into the night, the halos around the lampposts, and I thought: so here I am. I'm in Marseille, it is the last time in my life that I'll be seeing this. I must never forget it, ever, even if I live to be as old as Mme. d'Aleu, the old blind woman who shared our apartment at 26 rue des Gavilliers. I must never forget any of it. So, I straightened up a bit, pushing myself up on the old suitcases, and I looked at the bodies stretched out along the platform, against the walls, and the people sitting on the benches, nodding off to sleep, wrapped in their blankets, and they looked like dead skins, cast-off piles of clothing. My eyes were burning, there was a dizzy feeling in my head; I could hear the sounds of breathing, heavy, deep, and I felt tears rolling down my cheeks, along my nose, dripping onto the suitcase, without knowing why those tears were coming. Mama shifted slightly in her sleep, she moaned, and I caressed her hair as you do with a child so they won't wake up. A ways off, the clock showed its wan face, its moon face, where the hours went by so slowly: one o'clock, two o'clock, two-thirty. I tried to find the Shepherd at the other end of the platform under the clock, but he'd disappeared. He too had become a dead skin, a cast-off piece of rag. So, with my cheek against the suitcase, I thought about everything that had happened, everything that would happen, just like that, slowly, following haphazard paths, like when you write a letter. I thought about my father when he left, the last image I had of him, tall, strong, his gentle face, his very black curly hair, the look in his eyes, as if he were excusing himself, as if he'd done something foolish. For an instant, he was there, he was kissing me, he was hugging me so tight in his arms I couldn't catch my breath and I was laughing and pushing him away a little. Then he was gone, while I slept, leaving only the image of that grave face, those eyes that were asking forgiveness.

I think of him. Sometimes I pretend that I believe he's the one we're going to see, the one we'll find at the end of this journey. I've been practicing at pretending for a long time, until I believe it. It's hard to explain. It's like the energy that flows between the magnet and the steel pen point. One minute the point moves, quivers. The next minute—so fast you can't even see it—the pen point is stuck to the magnet. I remember when I was ten—it was at the beginning of the war—and we had fled Nice to go to Saint-Martin, that summer my father took me down into the valley to see the harvest, maybe it was the very place I went back to three years later with the Gasparini boy. We traveled the whole way in a horse cart and my father helped the farmers cut the wheat and tie it up in sheaves. I stayed close behind him, I breathed in the smell of his sweat. He'd taken off his shirt and I saw the tensed muscles on each side of his back under the white skin, like ropes. All of a sudden, in spite of the sunshine, in spite of the people shouting and the smell of the cut wheat, I knew that it would all come to an end, the thought was very vivid: my father would have to go away, forever, just as we are doing now. I remember, the idea crept up very quietly, hardly making a flutter, then suddenly it swooped down on me, squeezing my heart in its claws, and I couldn't keep on acting as if nothing had happened. Horror-struck, I ran down the path through the wheat, under the blue sky, I ran away as fast as I could. I wasn't able to scream or cry, all I could do was run with all my might, feeling the tight grip crushing my heart, smothering me. My father started running after me, he caught up with me on the road, he swept me up in his arms, tore me off the ground, I remember, and I, I was struggling, he hugged me very hard against his chest, trying to calm my tearless sobbing, my hiccups, stroking my hair and my neck. Afterward, he never asked me a single question, he didn't reprimand me. When people asked him what had happened, he simply said, nothing, nothing, she was just frightened. But I could see in his eyes that he understood, that he'd felt it too, the passing of that cold shadow, despite the lovely noon light and the golden wheat.

I remember once too, Mama and I went out for a walk one day over by Berthemont, we followed the sulfur stream up above the ruins of the hotel. My father had left ahead of us, he'd met up with the people in the Maquis, it was all very mysterious. There had been an exchange of notes that my father read hastily and then burned immediately, and Mama had gotten dressed hurriedly. She took me by the hand, we walked quickly along the deserted road by the river till we reached the abandoned hotel. First taking a small staircase, then up a narrow path, we began climbing the mountain, Mama was walking fast without getting winded and I had a hard time keeping up with her, but I didn't dare say anything because it was the first time I had gone with her. She had that impatient look on her face that I never run across nowadays, her eyes were shining feverishly. Then we walked on a very high slope covered with immense pastures, and the sky was all around us. I had never been up so high, so far away, before, and my heart was beating fast, from the effort, from feeling anxious. Afterward we reached the top of the slope and there, at the foot of the peaks, was a vast grassy plain, scattered with shepherds' huts of black drystone. Mama walked over to the closest huts and when we reached them, my father appeared. He was standing in the midst of the tall grasses, he looked like a hunter. His clothes were torn and dirty and he was carrying a rifle slung across his shoulder. I could hardly recognize him because his beard had grown out and his face was suntanned. As usual, he picked me up in his arms and hugged me very hard. And then he and Mama lay down in the grass near the hut and talked. I heard them talking, and laughing, but I stayed a little off to one side. I was playing with pebbles, I remember, tossing them onto the back of my hands like jacks.

I can still hear their voices and laughter that afternoon in the immense sloping pasture with the sky all around us. The clouds were rolling, describing dazzling scrolls on the blue of the sky, and I could hear the laughter and the snatches of my mother's and father's voices near me in the grass. And it was then, at that moment, that I realized my father was going to die. The idea dawned on me, and, try as I might to push it away, it came back, and I could hear his voice, his laughter, I knew that all I had to do was turn around to see them, to see his face, his hair and his beard shining in the sun, his shirt, and the shape of Mama lying next to him. And suddenly I threw myself to the ground and bit my hand to keep from screaming, to keep from crying, and in spite of myself I felt tears slipping out of me, emptiness gnawing in my stomach, making an opening to the outside, emptiness, coldness, and I couldn't stop thinking that he was going to die, that he had to die.

That's what I must forget on this journey, just as Uncle Simon Ruben said, "You must forget, you must go away to forget!"

Here, on the shores of Alon Bay, it all seems so far away, as if it had happened to someone else, in some other world. The strong north wind is blowing in the night and I'm lying very close against Mama, with Uncle Simon Ruben's stiff blanket pulled all the way up to my eyes. It's been so long since I've slept. My whole body aches, my eyes sting. The sound of the sea is reassuring, even if there is a storm. This is the first time I've spent the night by the sea. From the window in the train, as I stood in the aisle next to Mama before we reached Marseille, I saw it for an instant in the twilight, glistening, rippling in the wind. Everyone was over on the same side of the car, trying to get a glimpse of the sea. Later, in the train headed for Bandol, I tried to catch sight of it, my forehead plastered up against the cold window, jostled by the bumps and curves. But there was nothing but darkness, sudden bursts of light, and the far-off lamps dancing like ship-lights in the night.

The train stopped at the station in Cassis and many people got off, men and women muffled in their coats, some with large umbrellas as if they were going for a walk on the boulevards. I looked out to try and see if the Shepherd had gotten off with them, but he wasn't on the platform. Then the train lumbered slowly away and the people standing on the platform gradually faded into the distance like ghosts; it was sad and a little funny at the same time, like tired birds, buffeted by the wind. Are they going to Jerusalem too? Or maybe they're going to Canada? But there's no way of knowing, you can't ask them. There are people listening, people who want to know, to keep us from leaving. That's what Simon Ruben said when he took us to the platform in the train station, "Don't talk with anyone. Don't ask anyone anything. There are people listening to you." He slipped a piece of paper into The Book of the Beginning, with the name and address of his brother in Nice, Edouard Ruben Furniture, Descente Crotti, that's where we should say we're going if the police stop us. Then we arrived in Saint-Cyr, and everyone got off. A man was waiting for us on the platform of the station. He grouped everyone together who were to embark upon the journey and we began walking down the road, guided by the beam of his flashlight all the way to Alon Harbor.

Now we're on the beach, in the shelter of the broken-down hut, waiting for daybreak. Maybe other people are trying to see, just as I am. They sit up straight, peering out ahead of them, trying to see the light of the ship in the darkness, they search the crashing sound of the sea, listening for the sound of sailors' voices calling out. The giant pines creak and crack in the wind, their needles make the sound of waves cutting past the prow of a boat. The boat that's supposed to be coming is Italian, like Angelo Donati. It's called the *Sette Fratelli*, which means Seven Brothers. The first time I heard that name I thought of the seven children lost in the forest in the tale of Little Tom Thumb. With a name like that it seems nothing can go wrong.

I remember when my father used to talk about Jerusalem, when he would explain all about the city in the evening, like a story before bedtime. He and Mama weren't believers. I mean, they believed in G__, but they didn't believe in the Jewish religion or in any other kind of religion. But when my father spoke of Jerusalem in the days of King David, he told extraordinary tales. I thought it must be the biggest and most beautiful city in the world, not like Paris in any case, because there surely weren't dark streets over there, or dilapidated buildings, or broken drainpipes, or smelly stairwells, or gutters in which armies of rats ran free. When you say Paris, some people think you're lucky—such a beautiful city! But in Jerusalem it was certainly different. What was it like? I had a hard time imagining it, a city like a cloud, with domes and steeples and minarets (my father said there were a lot of minarets), surrounded by hills planted with orange and olive trees, a city that floated over the desert like a mirage, a city in which there was nothing commonplace, nothing dirty, nothing dangerous. A city in which everyone spent his time praying and dreaming.

I don't think I really knew what praying meant back then. Maybe I thought it was like dreaming, when you let secret things creep around you—what you want and love most in the world—just before dropping off to sleep.

Mama often talked about it too. The last days in Paris she lived for that one word alone, Jerusalem. She didn't really talk about the city, or the land, Eretz Israel, but about everything that had once existed over there, about everything that would begin again. For her, it was an open door, that's what she said.

The cold wind is slowly slipping inside of me, going straight through me. It's a wind that isn't coming from the sea, but blowing down from the north, over the hills, it's whistling through the trees. Now the sky is graying, I can see the very tall trunks of the trees and the sky appears between the branches. But the sea still isn't visible. Mama woke up because of the dawn chill. I can feel her body shivering next to mine. I hold her closer to me. I say words to soothe her. Did she hear me? I'd like to talk to her about everything, about the door, tell her it's really a very difficult and slow process, getting through that door. I feel as though she is the child and I, her mother. The journey began so long ago. I can remember each stage, from the very beginning. When we went to live in Paris in Simon Ruben's apartment on rue des Gravilliers with the old blind woman. That was when I stopped talking, stopped eating, except when Mama fed me with a spoon like a baby. I'd become a baby, I wet the bed every night. Mama put diapers on me that she made from old rags of different colors. There was a void after Saint-Martin, after walking through the mountains to Italy, the long walk all the way to Festiona. Memories came back to me in shreds, like the long wisps of fog trailing over the roofs of the village, and the shadows rising in the valley in winter. Hiding in the room in the Passagieri boarding house, I heard the dogs barking, heard the slow sound of the orphans' footsteps heading toward the dark church every evening, still heard Brao's voice yelling, "Elena!" while the schoolmaster was shoving him around by the shoulder. And the valley that opened all the way out to the icy window, the long rust-colored slopes that I'd searched, the empty paths with only the wind that carried with it the forge-like sounds of the villages, the faint shouts of children, nothing but the wind blowing right into the center of my being, hollowing out the emptiness within. Uncle Simon Ruben tried everything. He tried prayer, he sent for the rabbi and a doctor to heal the emptiness in me. The only thing he didn't try was the hospital, because Mama wouldn't have agreed to that or to his requesting help from the Social Services either. Those were the terrifying years that I left behind, in the cold shadows, the hallways, and the stairwells of rue des Gravilliers. They are fading away now, slipping by me backwards like the landscape past the train.

Never has a night seemed so long to me. I remember in the old days, before Saint-Martin, I used to wait uneasily for night to come because I thought that was when you could die, I thought that death stole people away in the night. You went to sleep alive and when night faded, you had disappeared. That's how Mme. d'Aleu died one night, leaving her cold white body in the bed, and Uncle Simon Ruben came to help Mama lay out the corpse for the funeral. Mama reassured me; she said that wasn't it at all, death didn't steal people away, it was simply that the body and mind were worn out and they just stopped living, as one goes to sleep. "And what about when someone is killed?" I asked that. I asked that and I was almost shouting and Mama averted her eyes as if she were ashamed at having lied, as if it were her fault. Because she'd also thought immediately of my father, and she said, "Those who kill others rob them of their lives, they are like wild animals, they are ruthless." She too was remembering when my father went off into the mountains with his rifle, she was remembering how he disappeared into the tall grasses, never to return again. When adults don't tell the truth, they look away because they're afraid that it will show in their eyes. But I was already cured of the emptiness by then, I wasn't afraid of the truth anymore.

Those nights are what I'm thinking about now in the gray light of dawn, as I listen to the sound of the sea on the rocks of Alon Bay. The ship should be coming soon to take us to Jerusalem. Those nights have all melted together, they've blotted out the days. In Saint-Martin the nights crept into my body, left me feeling cold, alone, and frail. Here on the beach with Mama's body lying close to mine and trembling, listening to her breathing mixed with little moaning sounds like a child's, I remember certain nights when we went home to 26 rue des Gravilliers—the cold, the sound of water in the drainpipes, the creaking sounds coming from the workshops in the courtyard, the voices echoing, and Mama lying next to me in the cold narrow room, holding me close to her body to keep me warm because my life was draining away from me, my life was leaking out into the sheets, into the air, into the walls.

I'm listening, and I think I can hear everyone who is waiting for the boat all around me. They're out there, lying in the sand against the wall of the ruined hut, under the tall pines sheltering us from the strong blustering wind. I don't know who they are; I don't know their names, except for the Shepherd, but that's just what I call him. They're nothing but faces barely visible in the semi-darkness, shapes, women muffled in their coats, old men hunched down under their wide umbrellas. All of them with the same suitcases wound with twine, with the same Red Cross or American Army blankets. Somewhere among them, the Shepherd, alone, still so much like an adolescent. But we mustn't talk to each other; we mustn't know anything. Simon Ruben said so, on the platform. He hugged Mama and me for a long time; he gave us a little money and his blessing. And so, we aren't the only ones to be going through that door. There are others here on this beach, and elsewhere, thousands of others who are waiting for boats that will sail away and never come back. They are sailing for other worlds, for Canada, South America, Africa, to places where perhaps people are waiting for them, where they can start a new life. But for those of us here on Alon beach, who is waiting for us? In Jerusalem, Uncle Simon Ruben would say with a laugh, only the angels are waiting for you. How many doors will we go through? Each time we crest the horizon, it will be like another door. To keep from losing hope, to resist the cold wind, the weariness, we must think about the city that is like a mirage, the city of minarets and domes shining in the sun, the dream city made of stone hovering over the desert. In that city we can surely forget. In that city there are no black walls, there's no black water trickling down, no emptiness or cold, or crushing crowds on the boulevards. We'll be able to live again, find what existed before, the smell of wheat in the valley near Saint-Martin, the water in the streams when the snow melts, the silent afternoons, the summer sky, the footpaths that disappear in the high grasses, the sound of the torrent and Tristan's cheek on my chest. I hate traveling, I hate time! It is life before destruction—that's what Jerusalem is. Is it really possible to find that by crossing the seas on the *Sette Fratelli*?

Day is breaking. For the first time, I'm able to think about what's in store for us. Soon the Italian boat will be out there in Alon Harbor, which I'm just now beginning to distinguish. It seems as if I can already feel the rolling of the sea. The sea will take us to that holy city, the wind will push us all the way to the door of the desert. I never spoke of G__ with my father. He didn't want us to talk about it. He had a way of looking at you, very simply and directly, that stopped you from asking questions. Afterwards, when he wasn't there anymore, it no longer mattered. One day Uncle Simon Ruben asked Mama if it wasn't time to start thinking about instruction—he meant religion—to make up for lost time. Mama always refused, without saying no but simply saying we'll see about that later, because it was against my father's wishes. She said it would come in time, when I was old enough to choose. She too believed that religion was a matter of choice. She didn't even want people to call me by my Jewish name, she said "Hélène" because it was also my name, the name she'd given me. But I called myself by my real name, Esther, I didn't want any other name now. One day my father told me the story of Esther, who was called Hadassa, and had neither father nor mother, and how she had married King Ahasuerus and dared to enter the grand chamber where the king was enthroned to ask him to save her people. And Simon Ruben told me about her, but he said the name of G__ should not be pronounced, or written, and that's why I thought it was a name that was like the sea, an immense name that was impossible to know in its entirety. So now I know it's true, I have to reach the other side, cross the sea, all the way to Eretz Israel and Jerusalem, I have to find that force. I never would have thought it was so huge, I never would have thought it was such a difficult door we had to go through. The fatigue, the cold prevent me from thinking about anything else. All I can think of is this interminable night that is now ending in a gray dawn, and the wind in the giant trees, and the sound of the sea between the sharp rocks. I drop off to sleep just then, lying close to Mama, listening to the wind flapping in the blanket like a sail, listening to the unbroken sound of the waves on the sandy beach. Perhaps I dream that when I open my eyes the ship will be out there on the sparkling sea.

I'm sitting in a cleft in the rocks next to a huge dead tree. I'm on the lookout. Before me, the sea is a blinding blue, it's painful to look at. The gusts of wind whip by overhead. I can hear them coming as they rush over the leaves of the bushes and through the branches of the pines, they make a liquid sound that blends in with the crashing of the waves on the white rocks. As soon as I woke up this morning, I ran out to the headland in Alon Harbor to get a better view of the sea.

Now the sun is burning my face, burning my eyes. The sea is so beautiful with its slow swell coming from the other side of the world. The waves beat against the coast, making a deep-water sound. I'm not thinking of anything now. I look out, my eyes tirelessly scanning the clear line of the horizon, searching the windswept sea, the naked sky. I want to see the Italian boat arrive, I want to be the first, when its prow cuts through the sea toward us. If I don't stay out here at the end of the promontory, at the entrance to Alon Bay, it seems as if the boat won't come. If I turn my eyes away for an instant, it won't see us, it will continue on its way to Marseille.

It has to be coming now, I can feel it. The sea can't be so beautiful, the sky can't have cast off all the clouds for no reason.

I want to be the first to shout when the boat appears. I didn't say anything to Mama when I left her on the beach still wrapped in the American blanket. No one came with me. I'm the lookout, my eyes are as sure and as sharp as those of the Indians in Gustave Aymard's novels. How I would love my father to be with me right now! Thinking of him, imagining him sitting next to me on the rocks, searching the sparkling sea, makes my heart beat faster and fills me with a sort of dizziness that blurs my vision. Hunger, tiredness might have a little something to do with it too. I haven't slept in so long, haven't really eaten! I feel as if I'm going to fall over headfirst into the dizzying black sea. I remember that's exactly how I used to watch the mountain shrouded in clouds where my father should have appeared. Every day in Festiona, I left the room in the boarding house and I went all the way to the top of the village from where I could see the whole valley and the whole mountain, the path coming out, and I looked and looked, so long, so hard, that I felt as if my eyes would bore a hole into the rocky cliff.

But I can't let myself go. I'm the lookout. The others are sitting on the beach waiting in the bend of Alon Bay. When I left this morning, Mama pressed my hand in hers without saying a word. The sun had come up and given her new strength. She smiled.

I want to see the Italian boat. I want it to come. The sea is immense, ablaze with light. The high wind rips the foam from the crests of the waves and throws it backward. The powerful rollers are coming from the other side of the world, dashing onto the white rocks, crowding against one another as they funnel into the narrow inlet of Alon Harbor. The blue water eddies inside the bay, sinking into whirlpools. Then it fans out on the shore.

The dead tree trunk is beside me. It's white and smooth as a bone. I'm very fond of that tree. I feel as though I've always known it. It's magic—thanks to it, nothing will happen to us. Insects scurry up the sea-worn trunk, through its roots. Sharpened by the hot sun, the pungent smell of pines drifts over on the wind. The wind keeps blowing, the sea is swirling, I think we're at the end of the earth, at the very limit, at the place where you can't turn back anymore, I think we're all going to die.

Dark cities, trains, fear, war, that's all behind us. Last night when we walked through the hills in the rain, guided by the flashlight, we were making our way through the first door. That's why everything was so hard, so tiring. The forest of giant pines at the back of Alon Bay, the sound of the branches cracking in the wind, the cold wind, the rain, and then the tumbled-down wall against which we all huddled like animals gone astray in a tempest.

I open my eyes, the sea and the light burn down into the very center of my body, but it feels good. I breathe in, I'm free. Already the wind, the waves, are whisking me away. The journey has begun.

I spent the whole day wandering around through the rocks on the headland. The sea always at my side, the line of the horizon in my mind. The wind is still blowing, whipping through the bushes, bowing the trunks of the trees. In the rocky recesses, there is holly, sarsaparilla. Near the sea some heather grows with small pink flowers stamped with black centers. The smells, the light, the wind give you a giddy feeling. The sea is churning.

On the beach in Alon Harbor, the emigrants are sitting next to one another, eating. For a minute, I sit down next to Mama, without taking my eyes from the line that separates the sky from the sea between the two rocky points. My eyes are burning, my face is on fire. The taste of salt is on my lips. I hurriedly eat the provisions that Mama has taken from her suitcase, a slice of white bread, a piece of cheese, an apple. I drink a lot of lemonade straight from the bottle. Then I go back to the rocks, to the lookout point, near the dead tree.

The sea is turbulent, ruffed with foam. It changes color constantly. When the clouds stretch over the sky again, it becomes gray, dark, violet, porphyry in fusion.

Now I'm cold. I curl up in the rock shelter. What are the others doing? Are they still waiting? If we lose faith, maybe the boat will turn around, stop struggling against the wind, head back to Italy. My heart is pounding hard and fast, my throat is dry because I know that our life is on the line at this very moment, that the *Sette Fratelli* isn't just any ship. It holds our destiny.

The Shepherd has come to see me in my hideout. It's already evening. Through a hole in the clouds, the sun shoots a harsh beam of light—purplish, as though it were mixed with ash. The Shepherd walks up to me, sits down on the tree trunk, talks to me. I don't listen to what he says at first, I'm too tired to chat. My eyes are burning, water is running from my eyes and nose. The Shepherd thinks I'm crying in discouragement, he sits next to me, puts his arm around my shoulders. It's the first time he's ever done that, I can feel the warmth of his body, see the light making the hairs of his beard shine strangely. I think of Tristan, the smell of his body wet from the river. It's a very old memory, from another life. It's as light as the shiver that is running over my skin. The Shepherd is talking, telling the story of his life, his mother and father taken to Drancy by the Germans, never to return. He says his name out loud, talks about what he will do in Jerusalem, what he would like to study—in America maybe—to become a doctor. He takes my hand and together we walk down to the harbor, down to the stone hut where the people are waiting. When I sit down again next to Mama, it's almost dark.

Little by little, the storm has returned. The clouds have hidden the stars. It's cold, rain is coming down in buckets.

We're wrapped in Uncle Simon Ruben's blanket, our backs against the crumbling wall. The giant pines have started creaking again. I feel a void whirling inside of me, I collapse. How will the boat be able to find us, now that there's no longer a lookout?

The Shepherd awakens me. He's leaning over me, he touches my shoulder, says something, and I must look so drowsy that he makes me get to my feet. Mama is standing too. The Shepherd points out a distant shape advancing on the sea, just in front of the inlet to Alon Harbor, barely visible in the gray light of dawn. It's the *Sette Fratelli*.

No one shouts, no one says anything. One after the other, men, women, children stand up on the beach, still wrapped in their blankets and coats, and gaze out to sea. The ship slowly enters the bay, its sails snapping in the wind. It veers, rolling on the waves that are hitting it broadside.

Just then, the clouds rip open. The sky shines between them and the dawn suddenly illuminates Alon Bay, its white rocks, glitters on the thick needles of the pines. There are sparkles out on the sea. The sails of the ship seem immense, white, almost unreal.

It's so beautiful we all have goosebumps. Mama has knelt down in the sand on the beach and other women do the same, then some men. I too am kneeling in the wet sand and we watch the ship anchor in the middle of the bay. We just watch. We can't speak anymore, can't think, can't anything. On the beach all the women are kneeling. They're praying, or weeping, I can hear their droning voices in the gusts of wind. Behind them, the old Jewish men have remained standing, dressed in their heavy black coats, some leaning on their umbrellas as if they were staffs. They are looking out to sea, their lips are moving too as if they were praying.

For the first time in my life I too am praying. It's within me, I can feel it, deep down inside, in spite of myself. It's in my eyes, in my heart, as if I were outside of my body and could see out beyond the horizon, beyond the sea. And everything I see right now has meaning, it's sweeping me along, casting me into the wind that blows over the sea. I have never felt that before: everything I've lived through, all the weariness, the long march through the mountains, then the horrible years spent in rue des Gravilliers, the years when I didn't even dare go out in the courtyard to see the sky, oppressive ugly years, and tedious—like a long illness, everything is being wiped away here in the glowing light of Alon Bay, with the *Sette Fratelli* drifting in slow circles around its anchor and the large white sails hanging slack and whipping in the wind.

We are all perfectly still, kneeling or standing on the beach, still wrapped in our blankets, numb with cold and sleepiness. We no longer have a past. We are brand new, as if we have just been born, as if we have slept a thousand years—here, on this beach. I say that out loud, the thought came to me in such a powerful flash that my heart is beating so hard I think it will burst. Mama is crying silently, from fatigue, maybe, or from happiness, I feel her body against mine slumping forward, as if she'd been beaten. Maybe she's crying because my father never came down the path where we were waiting for him. She hadn't cried then, even when she realized he would never come. And now there is the emptiness, the emptiness in the form of a boat, sitting still in the middle of the bay, and it's more than she can bear.

Is it a real boat, with men aboard? We look upon it with as much fear as longing, afraid that at any minute it will hoist anchor and sail out to sea on the wind, abandoning us on this deserted beach.

So the children start running over the sandy beach, they've forgotten about being tired, hungry, and cold. They run out to the rocky point waving their arms, shouting, "Hey! Heyo!" Their shrill voices pull me from my daydream.

It really is the *Sette Fratelli*, the ship we've been waiting for, the ship that will take us across the sea, all the way to Jerusalem. Now I remember why I so liked the boat's name, the first time Simon Ruben said it, the "seven brothers." One day, my father and I talked about Jacob's children, who are scattered all over the world. I don't remember all their names but I loved two of them because they were full of mystery. One was called Benjamin, the voracious wolf. The other was Zabulon, the sailor. I thought about how he'd disappeared with his ship in a storm one day and the sea had taken him off to another land. There was also Nephtali, the doe, and I fancied that my mother must resemble him because her eyes were so black and so gentle (and I as well, with my elongated eyes, always on the lookout). So maybe it was Zabulon who was coming back today on his ship to take us to the shores of our ancestors, after having roamed the seas for so very many centuries. The Shepherd is next to me, he takes my hand for a minute, without saying anything. His eyes are bright, his throat must be so tight with emotion that he can't talk. But as for me, I suddenly break away, and without waiting another instant, I start running over the beach with the children, and shouting, and waving my arms. The cold wind makes tears run from my eyes, tousles my hair. I know very well that Mama won't approve, but too bad! I have to run, I can't sit still anymore. I too must shout. So I shout whatever comes to mind, I wave my arms and shout to the ship, "Heyo! Zabulon!" The children get the idea too and they shout along with me, "Zabulon! Zabulon! Heyo, Zabulon!" in their shrill voices that sound like the cries of angry birds.

The miracle takes place: a rowboat with two crewmen aboard breaks away from the *Sette Fratelli*. It slips over the calm waters of the harbor and reaches the beach, greeted by the shouts of the children. One of the sailors jumps out. The children fall quiet, a little intimidated. The sailor looks at us for a minute, the women still kneeling, the old Jewish men in black coats, with their umbrellas. He has a red face, red hair matted with salt. The seven brothers are not the children of Jacob.

The storm rises again when we are all in the belly of the ship. From the hatches, I watch the sky changing, the clouds closing back up. The gray sails (seen close up they don't look so white) flap in the wind. They stretch taut, quivering, then fall slack again with sharp snapping sounds as if they were going to rip apart. Despite the engine chugging away in the hold, the *Sette Fratelli* is barely creeping along, it is leaning to one side, leaning so low that everyone has to cling to the frame of the hold to keep from tumbling around. I lie down next to Mama on the planking, my feet jammed up against the suitcases. Most of the passengers are already seasick. In the dim light of the hold, I see their shapes stretched out on the floor, their wan faces. The Shepherd must be sick too because he's disappeared. Those who can are leaning over toward the bottom of the hold, over the water, and are vomiting. Some children are crying in strangely feeble and high-pitched voices that mingle with the creaking of the hull and the whistling of the wind. There is the sound of voices too, murmurs, entreaties, complaints. I think everyone regrets having been trapped on this boat, this tiny nutshell tossing about on the sea. Mama isn't complaining. When I look at her, she smiles faintly but her face is dirt-colored. She tries to speak, she says, "Star, little star," just as my father used to. But the next minute I have to help her crawl over to the waterway. Then she stretches out afterward and she is cold all over. I press her hand very tightly in mine, the way she used to do when I was sick...Up on the deck, the crewmen are dashing back and forth barefoot in the storm, they're shouting and cursing in Italian, grappling and thrashing about as if curbing a mad horse.

The engine stopped, but I didn't notice it right away. The boat is pitching and rolling so much it's terrifying, and all of a sudden it strikes me that we're going to capsize. I can't stand being shut in with all of this happening. Despite it being strictly forbidden, despite the gale winds and the driving rain, I push open the hatch and stick my head out.

In the dim light of the storm, I see the sea rush toward the boat, explode in a deluge of white spume. The wind has become an invisible monster, it pounds against the sails, jerks at them, leans against the two masts and tips the boat sideways. The wind whirls, it smothers me, forces tears from my eyes. I try to resist so I can watch the sea, so beautiful, so terrifying. One of the sailors motions for me to go back down into the hold. He's a young boy with very black hair, he's the one who helped us get settled in the hold when we boarded. He speaks French. He makes his way toward me, clinging to the rail. He shouts, "Go back down! Go back down! It's dangerous!" I shake my head no, signal to him that I don't want to, that I'll be sick down below, that I'd rather stay on deck. I tell him we're probably going to die and that I want to meet death face to face. He stares at me, "Are you crazy? Get down below or I'll tell the captain." I scream, against the wind, against the deafening roar of the sea, "Leave me alone! We're all going to die! I don't want to go down there!" The young boy points to a dark patch on the sea out in front of the ship. An island. "We're going over there! We're going to wait out the storm! We're not going to die! Now get down below!" The island is straight ahead, less then two hundred meters from us. Already, it is protecting the ship, the wind has stopped pushing against the masts. Water floods over the deck, gushes down the planking, streams from the sails hanging from the yards. Suddenly everything is silent, with the crashing of the sea still echoing in our eardrums. "Then it's true, we're not going to die?" I say that in such a way it makes the young sailor burst out laughing. He pushes me politely toward the hatch just as the other crewmen appear, haggard. Overhead the sky is ablaze. "What's the name of this island? Are we already in Italy?" The young boy simply says, "It's Port-Cros Island, in France, Mademoiselle. This is Port-Man Bay." So I go back down into the belly of the ship. There is a stale smell, I can sense the fear, the anxiety. Groping in the shadows, I look for Mama. "It's over now. We've reached Port-Man. It's our first stopover." I say that as if we were on a cruise. I'm exhausted. Now I lie down on the wooden planking too. Mama is next to me, she puts her hand on my forehead. I close my eyes.

We've been in the bay of Port-Man for a day and a night now, not doing anything. The ship is drifting slowly around on its moorings, first in one direction, then in the other. The hold echoes with the sound of tools repairing the engine. Even though the captain (a fat bald man who looks like anything but a seaman) has forbidden it, I go up on deck all the time with the other children. I'm thin, and with my short hair, I believe I can pass for a boy. We go to the poop, amid the rigging. I sit down and gaze at the black shore of the island under the stormy skies. The coast is so close I'd have no trouble swimming that far. In Port-Man Bay the water is smooth and clear, despite the rainy sky and gusting winds.

The young Italian sailor comes over and sits down beside me. Sometimes he talks to me in Italian, other times in French, or in English mixed with a few Italian words. He tells me his name is Silvio. He offers me an American cigarette. I try smoking it, but it's harsh and sweet and it makes my head spin. Then he takes a bar of chocolate out of his jacket pocket and breaks off a row of squares for me. The chocolate is sweet and bitter at the same time, I don't believe I've ever eaten anything like that before. The boy goes through all of these motions gravely, without smiling, watching the ladder to the bridge where the captain might appear. "Why don't you let people come up on deck?" I ask slowly, staring at him. "It's very uncomfortable down there, it's stuffy and dark. It's inhuman." Silvio seems to think it over. He says, "The captain doesn't like it. He doesn't want anyone to see that there are passengers on board. It's forbidden." I say, "But we're not doing anything wrong. We're going to our country." He puffs nervously on his cigarette. He looks over toward the Island, the dark forest, and the small white beach. He says, "If the customs officers come, they'll stop the ship. We won't be able to leave." He throws his cigarette into the water and gets up, "Now you have to go back down into the hold." I call the other children and we go back inside the boat. In the hold it is hot and dark. There is a din of voices. Mama squeezes my arm, her eyes are glassy. "What were you doing? Whom were you talking to?" The men are talking loudly at the other end of the hold. There is anger or fear in their voices. Mama murmurs, "They say we aren't going any farther, that we've been tricked, that they're going to make us get out here."

We watch the light coming from the hatch all day long, a gray painful light. We can see the clouds going by, shrouds veiling the sky, as if night were falling. Gradually the men fall silent. Up on deck the crewmen stop working. We hear the rain pattering on the hull. I dream that we are far out at sea, in the middle of the Atlantic, and that the two of us are sailing to Canada. Long ago in Saint-Martin, that was where she wanted to go. I remember her talking about Canada in winter—in the little room where I waited wide-eyed in the dark—the snow, the forests, the wooden houses on the banks of endless rivers, the flight of wild geese. That's what I'd like to hear about now. "Tell me about Canada." Mama leans toward me, kisses me. But she doesn't say anything. Maybe she's too tired to think about a country that doesn't exist. Maybe she's forgotten.

During the night the storm starts up again. The waves must be washing over the rocky headland that shields Port-Man, they're crashing against the ship, making it sway and creak and everyone wakes up. We're holding onto the frame to keep from being tossed against the hull. The bundles, the suitcases, other invisible objects slide around and knock against the walls of the ship. We can't hear a single voice, not a human sound on deck, and soon the rumor spreads: the crew has abandoned us, we're alone aboard the ship. Before fear can take root, the men light a storm lantern. Everyone gathers around the lamp, the men on one side, the women and children on the other. I see the faces lit up fantastically, eyes shining. One of the men comes from Poland, his name is Reb Joel. He's tall and thin with beautiful hair and a black beard. Sitting in front of the lamp, he lays a small black box tied with a thong down next to him. He recites strange words in that language I don't understand. He slowly pronounces the words that resound—the rough, long, mellow words—and I recall the voices chanting long ago in the temple in the house in Saint-Martin. No words have ever had that effect on me, like something tingling in my throat, like a memory. "What is he saying?" I ask Mama in a whisper. The men and women are rocking slowly in unison with the movement of the ship in the storm, and Mama is rocking too, watching the flame of the lamp on the floor. "Listen, it's our language now." She says that and I look at her face. The rabbi's words are powerful, they ward off the fear of death. On the planking, the little black leather box shines strangely, as if it encloses some incomprehensible force. The men's and the women's voices join Joel's words and I try to read their lips to understand. What are they saying? I'd like to ask Jacques Berger, but I don't dare go and sit next to him, I might break the spell, and fear would settle back down upon us. They are words that go with the movement of the sea, words that rumble and roll, gentle and powerful words, words of hope and of death, words that are bigger than the world, more powerful than death. When the ship arrived in Alon Bay at dawn, I learned what prayer was. Now I listen to the words of the prayer, the language carries me along on its tide. Reb Joel's words echo through the boat for me as well. I'm not an outsider, I'm not a foreigner. The words sweep me along, take me off to another world, to another life. Now I know, I understand. Joel's words will take us there, all the way to Jerusalem. Even if there is a storm, even if we have been abandoned, we'll reach Jerusalem with the words of the prayer.

The children have gone back to sleep, lying close to their mothers. Grave or melodious voices echo the words of Joel, follow the rhythm of the waves. Perhaps they are commanding the wind, the rain, the night. The flame of the lamp wavers, makes eyes shine. Next to Reb Joel, the little black box gleams oddly, as if the words were coming from it.

I lie back down on the floor. I'm not afraid anymore. Mama's hand runs through my hair, just like in the old days, I hear her voice repeating the words in my ear, the rough mellow words of the prayer. It lulls me to sleep. Now I'm back in my memories, the oldest memories on earth.

As it was sailing out of Port-Man this morning at dawn, customs officers boarded the *Sette Fratelli*. The sea was calm, nice and smooth after the storm. The ship's engine had been repaired and it was headed out to sea in full sail. I was on deck with several children, watching the deep sea opening out before us. And suddenly, before anyone had time to realize what was happening, the patrol boat appeared. Its powerful prow cut through the sea, it came up alongside us. For a second, the captain pretended he didn't understand, and the *Sette Fratelli*, leaning into the wind, continued cresting the waves as it made its way out to sea. Then the customs officers shouted something from the loud speaker. It was unequivocal.

I watched the patrol boat approach. My heart started beating wildly, I couldn't take my eyes off the men in uniform. The captain gave some orders and the Italian crew lowered sail and stopped the engine. Our ship began to drift. Then, following orders, we turned our back on the open sea and headed toward the coast. The still-dark shoreline lies before us. We're not sailing for Jerusalem anymore. The words of the prayer are no longer bearing us along. We're heading for the large port of Toulon where we'll be put in prison.

In the belly of the ship no one is saying anything. The men are sitting in the same place as they were yesterday, like so many ghosts. The children are still sleeping for the most part, their heads lying on their mother's laps. The others have come down from the deck, hair rumpled from the wind. In a corner of the hold near the luggage, the storm lamp has gone dark.

They've shut us up in this large empty room, at the very end of the shipyards in the arsenal, probably because they couldn't put us in cells with the ordinary prisoners. They gave us cots, blankets. They took all of our papers, money, and anything that could serve as a weapon, even the women's knitting needles and the men's little scissors for trimming their beards. Through the tall barred windows we can see a barren lot covered with cracked cement where tufts of grass wave in the wind. At the end of the lot, there is a high stone wall. If it weren't for that wall, we could see the Mediterranean and dream that we would soon be on our way. Two days after they locked us up in the arsenal, I wanted so badly to get a glimpse of the sea that I worked out a plan to escape. I didn't tell anyone about it because Mama would be worried and then I wouldn't have had the heart to make a break for it. At lunchtime, three marines enter our room through the door at the far end. Two distribute the rations of soup while the third one stands watch, leaning on his rifle. I was able to get near the door without raising any suspicions. When one of the marines handed me the dish full of soup, I dropped it on his feet and escaped, running down the corridor, paying no attention to the shouts behind me. I ran like that, with all my might and I was so fast and so light on my feet that no one could have caught me. At the end of the corridor was the door that opens onto the lot. I ran out into the open air without stopping. I hadn't seen the sunshine in so long it made my head swim and I could feel my heart

pounding in my neck, in my ears. The sky was bright blue—
not a cloud—everything was shining in the cold air. I ran all
the way to the high stone wall looking for a way out. The
cold air was stinging my throat and my nose, making my
eyes water. I stopped for an instant to look over my shoulder.
But it seemed as if no one was following me. The lot was
empty, the high walls shone. It was mealtime and all the
marines must have been in the mess hall. I ran along the wall
without stopping. Suddenly, right in front of me, there was
the huge gate open on both sides and the avenue that led out
to the sea. I went through the gate as quick as an arrow, not
knowing whether there was a guard in the sentry box. I ran
without stopping to catch my breath down to the end of the
avenue where there is a fort and some rocks looking out over
the sea. Now I'm in the brush, hands and legs full of
scratches, jumping from rock to rock. I haven't forgotten
how to do it since Saint-Martin, when I used to go up the
torrent. In a split second I spot the place I'll jump to, the line
of approach I can take, the holes to avoid. Afterward the
rocks get steeper, I have to slow down. I cling to the brush,
climb to the very bottom of the crevices.

When I reach the point just above the sea, the wind is
blowing so hard that I can barely breathe. The wind pushes
me against the rocks, whistles through the brush. I stop in a
hollow in the rocks, and the sea is directly below me. It's as
beautiful as it was in Alon Harbor, a vast fiery stretch,
smooth and hard, with the dark masses of the capes and
peninsulas in the distance. The wind whirls around at the
entrance to my hiding place, it growls and whines like an
animal. Down below, the foam leaps against the rocks,
scatters in the wind. There is nothing here but the wind and
the sea. Never have I felt so free. It makes your head spin, it
makes you shudder. Then I look out to the line of the horizon

as if our ship would appear on the blazing path that the sun is making on the sea. My thoughts carry me to the other side of the world, I've traversed the wind and gone over the sea, I have left behind the black piles of capes and islands where humans dwell, where they imprisoned us. Like a bird, I skim out on the wind over the sea in the sunlight and the salt spray, I've abolished time and distance, I've reached the other side, the place where land and men are free, where everything is truly new. I'd never thought of that before. It's inebriating, because right now I'm not thinking of Simon Ruben anymore, or of Jacques Berger, or even of my mother, I'm no longer thinking of my father who disappeared in the tall grasses up above Berthemont, I'm not thinking of the boat anymore, or of the marines who are looking for me. Only— is anyone really looking for me?

Mightn't I have disappeared forever, suspended in my rocky hiding place, my bird's lair, up over the waves with my eyes fixed on the sea? My heart is beating slowly, I don't feel afraid anymore, I don't feel hungry, or thirsty, I don't feel the weight of the future anymore. I'm free, the freedom of the wind, of light, is now within me. It's the first time.

I stay in my hiding place all day, watching the sun sinking slowly toward the sea. No one comes. I've wanted to be really alone for so long now, without anyone talking next to me. I think of the mountains, the huge valley, the window of ice when I was watching for my father to return. It's the image that I've carried with me wherever I went when I needed to be alone. It's the image that came to me when I was shut up in the dark room on rue de Gravilliers, it would appear on the wallpaper. I still remember. My father walking through the grass in front of me, and the stone huts where Mama and I came up. The silence, only the sound of the wind in the grass. Their laughter while they were kissing. Just like here, the silence, the wind whistling in the brush, the cloudless sky, and the far end of the vast misty valley and the cones of the peaks sticking up like islands. I kept it all with me, in my head the whole time—in Simon Ruben's garage, in the apartment on rue des Gravilliers where we never went out, even when Simon Ruben said the Germans wouldn't come back, they would never come back. The mountain was in my head then, the grassy slope that seemed to rise all the way up to the sky, and the valley lost in mist, the thin trails of smoke that drifted up from the villages in the clear air at twilight.

That's what I want to remember, not the horrid sounds, the shots. I am walking along as if in a dream and Mama squeezes my arm. She shouts, "Come on, honey, come on, run! Run!" And she drags me by the arm down toward the bottom of the mountain as fast as she can, through the grass that cuts my lips, and I run out in front of her in spite of my trembling knees, with that strange voice of hers in my ears that cracks when she screams, "Run! Run!"

Here in my hiding place, for the first time it seems as though I might never again hear those sounds, those words, as though I'll never see those dream images again, because the wind, the sun, and the sea are inside of me and have washed it all away.

I stay in my hiding place among the rocks until the sun almost reaches the horizon and is touching the line of trees on the peninsula across the harbor.

Then I suddenly feel the cold. It settles in with the night. Maybe it's because I'm hungry and thirsty too, because I'm so very weary. I feel as though I haven't stopped walking and running ever since the day we came down from the mountain through the tall grasses that cut my lips and my legs and since that day my heart hasn't stopped beating so hard and so fast, pounding in my chest like a frightened animal. Even in the dark apartment on rue de Gravilliers, I never stopped walking and running, I never caught my breath. The doctor who came to see me was named Rose, I haven't forgotten his name even though I only saw him once, because I heard Mama and Uncle Simon Ruben saying that extraordinary name, "Mr. Rose said...Mr. Rose went...Mr. Rose thinks..." When he came, when he walked into our shabby apartment, I thought everything would brighten up, start shining. Yet I wasn't really disappointed when I saw that Mr. Rose was a pudgy little bald man, with thick nearsighted glasses. He examined me through my clothing, he felt my neck and my arms and he said I had asthma, that I was too thin. He gave us some eucalyptus tablets for my asthma; he told Mama that I needed to eat meat. Meat! Did he have any idea that all we ate were overripe vegetables that Mama found discarded at the market, and sometimes only peelings? But from then on I had broth made with chicken necks and feet that Mama bought twice a week. After that, I never saw Mr. Rose again.

I think about all of that when night falls in the harbor because it seems like here in this hiding place, I've stopped walking and running for the first time. My heart has finally started beating calmly in my chest, I can breathe with no difficulty, without making my lungs wheeze.

The dogs awakened me before daybreak. The marines found me in my cave, they brought me back to the arsenal. When I walked into the large room, Mama got up from her bed, she walked over to me, kissed me. She didn't say anything. I couldn't say anything to her either, not why, not that I was sorry. I knew I would never have another day and night like that again. It was still inside of me along with the sea, the wind, the sky. Now they could put me in prison forever.

No one said anything. But the people who'd ignored me up to then now spoke to me in a kind way. The Shepherd came over to sit down beside me, he spoke to me in a polite way that seemed odd. It seemed as if years had passed over there in my hiding place in the rocks. We sat there on the floor talking all day long by the tall windows. Reb Joel came over to join us too, he talked about Jerusalem, about the history of our people. I liked it most when he talked about the religion.

Neither my father nor my mother had ever spoken to me about religion. Uncle Simon Ruben talked about the religion sometimes, about ceremonies, holidays, marriages. But for him they were ordinary things, not frightening, not mysterious, just routine. And if I asked him a question about religion, he got angry. He knitted his brow, looking at me askance, and Mama just stood still, as if she felt guilty. It's because my father wasn't a believer, he was a communist, according to what people say. So Uncle Simon Ruben didn't dare send for the rabbi, and he spoke angrily about the religion.

But when the Shepherd spoke of religion with Reb Joel, he really turned into another person. I loved listening to them, and I shot furtive glances in their direction, the Shepherd with his golden hair and beard and Joel with his very white face, his black hair, his slim body. His eyes were a very pale green, like Mario's, I thought he was the one who was truly the shepherd.

It was odd, talking about the religion like that in this large room where we were prisoners. The Shepherd and Joel talked in low voices to avoid disturbing the others, and it was as if we were still prisoners in Egypt, as if we were soon going to leave, and the terrifying voice would echo in the heavens and in the mountains and the light would shine in the desert.

I think I asked stupid questions, because I didn't know anything. My father had never talked to me about all of that. I asked why G__ is ineffable, why he is invisible and hidden, since he created everything on earth. Reb Joel shook his head, saying, "He isn't invisible, he isn't hidden. It is we who are invisible and hidden, it is we who are in the darkness." He said that often, "the darkness." He said that religion is the light, the only light, and that the lives of human beings, their acts, all the grand and magnificent things they build are nothing but darkness. He said, "He who created everything is our father, we are his offspring. Eretz Israel is our birthplace, the place where the first light shone, where the first shades of darkness began."

We were sitting by the window and I was staring at the deep blue sky. "We'll never get to Jerusalem." I said that because I was tired of thinking about it. I wanted to go back to my hiding place in the rocks over the sea. "Maybe Jerusalem doesn't even exist?" The Shepherd shot a furious glance at me. His gentle face was tense with anger. "Why do you say that?" He spoke slowly, but his eyes were bright with impatience. I said, "Maybe it exists, but we'll never get there. The police won't let us leave. We'll have to go back to Paris." The Shepherd said, "Even if they prevent us from leaving today, we'll go tomorrow. And if they prevent us from taking the boat, we'll go on foot, even if we have to walk for a year." He wasn't saying that because he wanted to get away, but because he too wanted to see the land where the religion began, where the first book was written. It made my heart speed up to see the light in his eye. Since he wanted so badly to go to Jerusalem, maybe we really would get there one day.

The days went by like that, long-drawn-out days that we forgot. People said they were going to take us to court and we'd be sent back to Paris. When I saw Mama dejected and sad, sitting on her bed staring at the floor, huddled up in her blanket because of the chill, it broke my heart. I said to her, "Don't be sad, sweet little Mama, you'll see, we'll get out. I have a plan. If they try and put us on a train for Paris, I have a plan, we'll make a getaway." It wasn't true, I didn't have a plan, and ever since my escape, the marines had been keeping a sharp eye on me. "And where would we go? They'd stop us again wherever we went." I squeezed her hands very hard. "You'll see, we'll follow the coast, we'll go to Nice, find Uncle Simon's brother. After that, we'll go to Italy, to Greece, and finally we'll reach Jerusalem." I didn't have the slightest idea which countries you had to cross to get to Eretz Israel, but the Shepherd had mentioned Italy and Greece. Mama was smiling a little. "Dear child! And where would we get the money for the journey?" I said, "Money? That's no problem, we'll work along the way. You'll see, with the two of us, we won't need anyone's help." After talking about it so much, I ended up believing it. If we couldn't find work, I'd sing in the streets and in the courtyards, with my face painted black and I'd wear white gloves like the minstrels in the streets of London, or else I'd learn how to walk a tightrope and I'd wear a suit covered with sequins and the passersby would throw coins into an old hat and Mama would always be there to keep an eye out because the world is full of bad people. I even pictured the Shepherd walking with us in Italy, and Reb Joel too, with his black clothing and his prayer box. He'd speak to people about the religion, he'd speak of Jerusalem. And people would sit down around him to listen, and they'd give us food and a little money, especially the women and the young girls, because of the Shepherd and his beautiful golden hair.

I had to work out a plan to save us. I spent my nights going over everything in my mind. I thought of every possible trick to escape the marines, the police. Maybe we could throw ourselves into the sea and swim through the waves with some sort of floating devices or on a raft till we got past the Italian border. But Mama didn't know how to swim and I wasn't sure whether the Shepherd did either, or whether Reb Joel would want to jump into the water with his fine black suit and his book.

Come to think of it, he wouldn't want to abandon his family here, leave his people in the hands of enemies who were holding us prisoner. We all had to get away, the old people, the women, the children, everyone who was imprisoned, because they deserved to go to Jerusalem too. Besides, Moses himself wouldn't have abandoned the others to run off to Eretz Israel by himself. That's really what was so difficult.

What I liked most about the large room where we were prisoners were the long afternoons, after the noon meal, when the sun shone on the high windows and burned off some of the cold dampness. The women settled down in the rectangles of light outlined on the gray stone floor, spreading blankets out as if they were carpets, and they chatted while the children played next to them. Their conversations made a strange humming sound like a beehive. The men stayed over at one end of the room; they talked in low voices, smoking and drinking coffee, sitting on the cots, and the sound of their voices made a deeper buzzing, punctuated by exclamations, bursts of laughter.

That's when I liked to listen to the stories that Reb Joel told. He came and sat down with the children on the ground, in the light from one of the windows, and his black hair and clothing shone like silk. At first Joel was only talking to the Shepherd and me, without raising his voice so as not to disturb the others. He opened his black book and read slowly, first in the language that was so beautiful, so rough and mellow, that I'd heard in the temple in Saint-Martin. Then he spoke in French, slowly, searching for words, and sometimes the Shepherd helped him because he didn't speak the language well. Afterwards, Mama came over too and other children, foreign girls and boys who didn't speak our language but who stayed anyway, listening. There was also a young girl whose name was Judith, dressed in rags, always with a flowered scarf on her head, like a peasant. We waited for Reb Joel to start talking and when he began, it was like an inner voice that was saying what we were hearing. He spoke of the law and of religion as if they were the simplest things in the world. In basic terms, he explained what the soul was—comparing it to our shadows—and justice—comparing it to the sunlight, the beauty of children. Then he picked up the Book of the Beginning, the one Uncle Simon Ruben had given Mama before our departure, and he explained what was written there. Nothing was better than the story of the beginning of the world. First he pronounced the words in the divine language, slowly, making each word and each syllable resound, and sometimes we thought we understood just from hearing the words of that language echoing out in the silence of our prison. Because then, everyone stopped the chattering and discussions and even the old men listened, sitting on their cots. They were the words of G__, the words he'd suspended in space before creating the world. Joel pronounced the name slowly in a breath, like this, "Elohim, Elohim, he alone amongst the others, the greatest of all beings, he who is himself and from himself, he who can create..." He read of the first days, in that large room with the rectangles from the windows slowly pivoting on the floor.

"Thus, in the beginning Elohim created the person heaven, the person earth."

I said, "Persons? The heaven and the earth were persons?"

"Yes, persons, the first creatures, in the image of Elohim." He read on, *"For the earth was being formed and darkness was in the void."* He said, "Elohim used the void, the void is the cement of the earth, of existence."

He resumed, *"And the spirit of the Almighty, Elohim, moved and cast seed over the face of the waters."* He said, "The spirit, the breath, over the cold water."

He spoke of the sun, of the moon, they were legends. We no longer thought about the darkness in the room, about time making the windows revolve on the floor.

It was wonderful. All of us, Judith, even the younger children understood immediately what his words meant.

He went on reading, "*He, the Almighty, said let there be light. And there was light. He, the Almighty, saw that it was good. He, the Almighty, divided the light from the darkness.*" Joel said, "The light was that which we could know, and the darkness was the cement of the earth. And so, both were given—divided for eternity, and impossible to keep united. On one side, intelligence, on the other, the world..."

"*And, he, the Almighty, called the light IOM, and the darkness he called LAYLA.*" We listened to those names, the most beautiful names we had ever heard. "IOM was like the sea, limitless, filling everything, giving everything. LAYLA was empty, the cement of the earth." I listened to the words of that holy language, echoing out in the prison. "*And it was the end of the day in the west and the dawn in the east. IOM EHED.*"

When Joel said that, Day One, it was like a tingling shiver: the first day, the birth of the world.

"*And he, the Almighty, said let there be a firmament in the midst of the waters. And the Almighty made the firmament dividing the waters below from the waters above. And it was so.*"

"What are the waters below?" I asked. Joel looked at me without answering. Finally he said, "Wait, the book does not speak for no reason. Listen to the rest, "*and he, the Almighty called the firmament SHAMAÏN, the heavens, the waters above, and the night came in the west, the dawn in the east. IOM SHENI.*" He waited a brief instant, then began again, "*And he, the Almighty, said let the waters under the heaven be gathered together unto one place, and let the dry land appear. And it was so.*"

brought more men, more women, more children to the camp.

Now I remember how our Aunt Houriya came to the camp. Even though she was no blood relation of mine and she arrived a few days after I did along with the refugees from al-Quds, I called her my aunt because I loved her as if she were a true relative. She'd come, just as I had, in a United Nations tarpaulined truck. Her only belonging was a sewing machine. Since she had no place to live, I took her into the shack of wooden planks where I was living alone, in the part of the camp that was at the foot of the rocky hill. When she got down from the truck—the last person to get off—the impression I got of her was the one that always remained with me, right up to the end—dignified, composed, amid all of us already exhausted from the hardships. She had a reassuring silhouette, standing nice and straight on the dusty ground. She was draped in a traditional garment, the long *galabieh* of light-colored cloth, the black *shirwal*, her face covered with a white veil, wearing sandals encrusted with copper on her feet. The newcomers gathered their bundles together and started walking toward the center of the camp to find shelter from the sun, a place to live. The foreigners' truck went back to Tulkarm in a cloud of dust. She stood there beside her sewing machine, very still, as if she were waiting for another truck that would take her still farther. Then, from among the youngsters who were staring at her, she chose me, maybe because I was the oldest. She said to me, "Show me the way, my child." That's what she said, she'd used the word *benti*, my child, and I think that's why I called her Aamma, aunt, as if she'd come to Nour Chams to see me, as if I had been waiting for her.

When she took off her veil in the shack, I liked her face straightaway. Her skin was a dark copper color and there was a strange gleam in her sea-green eyes, as if they held a special light, something peaceful and disquieting at the same time. Maybe she was able to see beyond things, beyond people, the way certain blind persons can.

Aamma moved into the shack where I was living alone. She put down the sewing machine wrapped in a few rags to protect it from the dust. She chose the part of the house nearest the door. She slept on the ground rolled up in a sheet that she would pull over her head and disappear into completely. During the day, when she had finished making the food, she sometimes used her sewing machine to repair people's clothing, and they paid her with whatever they could, food, cigarettes, but never money, because in our camp money was of no use at all. She did that for as long as she had thread. The women brought her bread, sugar, tea or sometimes olives. But sometimes they had nothing to give her but thanks, and that was enough.

Nights were especially wonderful, because of the stories. Sometimes, just like that, without our knowing why, at the end of the afternoon, when the sun went down and disappeared behind the mist gathering in the west, in the direction of the sea, or on the contrary, when the wind swept the clouds away and the sky was resplendent, with the crescent moon hanging in the night like a saber, Aamma Houriya began to tell a Djinn story. She knew, she felt it in her bones, that it was the right evening to tell the tale. She sat down in front of me, and her eyes shone out eerily as she said, "Listen, I'm going to tell you a Djinn story." She knew all about the Djenoune, she'd seen them, like red flames dancing on the desert at night. You never saw them in the daytime, they hid in the bright sunlight. But at night, they appeared. They lived in cities, like human cities, with towers and ramparts, cities with ornamental lakes and gardens. She alone knew where those cities were, and she even promised to take me there when the war was over.

So, she started to tell a story. She sat down in the doorway to our shack, facing outward, not wearing a veil, because she wasn't telling the story just for me. I sat inside the house, in the shadows, very close to her so I could hear her voice.

Then the neighbor children arrived, one after the other. They passed the word on from one to another, and they sat down in front of the house in the dust, or they remained standing, leaning against the wall of boards. When Aamma Houriya started telling a Djinn story, she had a different voice, a new voice. It wasn't her everyday voice anymore, but one that was more hushed, deeper, that forced us to keep quiet in order to hear her better. Evenings, there was not a sound in the camp. Her voice was like a murmur, but we could hear every word, and we didn't forget them.

Aamma Houriya's face changed too, gradually. To hear better, I stretched out on the floor near the door, and I watched her face come to life. Her eyes shone even more, shot out sparks. She mimed expressions, she showed her frightened face, her angry face, her jealous face. She mimicked voices, deep and muffled, or sharp, strident, and even whimpering. Her hands made motions, as if she were dancing, making her copper bracelets jangle. But the rest of her body was motionless, sitting with her legs crossed in the doorway.

The stories Aamma Houriya told us, sitting in the dust in front of the shack as the light grew softer, were beautiful tales. They were stories that frightened us, about men who turn into wolves when they cross a river, or about dead people who come up out of their graves to breathe. Stories of spirits, of ghost cities lost somewhere in the desert, and travelers who go astray and happen to enter one of those cities, and never come back. Stories about a Djinn who marries a woman, or of a Djenna who captures a man and drags him to her house high in the mountains. When the desert wind blows, an evil Djinn enters the bodies of children and makes them lose their minds, makes them climb up on the roofs of houses as if they were birds, or makes them jump into deep wells as if they were toads.

She also told us stories of the evil eye, when Bayrut, the sorceress, bewitches the mother of a young child and makes her believe she is her aunt.

The young woman turns her back for a minute and Bayrut takes the child and puts a large stone wrapped in blankets in its place in the cradle, then she cooks the child and serves the baby to its own mother for dinner. Then Aamma showed us how we could resist the evil eye by putting our hands in front of our faces and writing the name of God on our forehead. She showed us how to scare witches away by blowing on a pinch of sand in the open palm of our hands. She also told stories of Aïsha the African, who was black and cruel—disguised as a slave, she ate the hearts of children to remain immortal. When Aamma Houriya took me by the hand and had me sit down next to her in front of the house, asking, "What will I tell you about tonight?" I immediately answered, "A story about old immortal Aïsha!"

I forgot who I was, where I was, I forgot about the three dry wells, the miserable hovels where men and women slept on the ground, awaiting the night, awaiting the unknown; I forgot about the starving children who stood watch on top of the rocky hill, waiting for the United Nations supply trucks to come, and who cried out when they saw the approaching cloud of dust, "Bread! Flour! Milk! Flour!" And the hard, bitter bread that was distributed in rations of two slices per person a day, and sometimes only one slice. I forgot about the sores that covered the children's bodies, the fleabites, the scabs from lice, the crevasses in their heels, their hair falling out by the handful, the conjunctivitis burning their eyelids.

Aamma Houriya didn't always tell us stories to frighten us. When she saw we were at the breaking point, that the children were exhausted and their faces were sunken from hunger, and that the scorching sun was unbearable, she said, "Today is a day for a water story, a garden story, a story of a city with fountains that sing and gardens full of birds."

Her voice was softer, her eyes shone with a gayer light and she began her story:

"Long ago you know, the earth wasn't what it is today. Both the Djenoune and human beings inhabited the earth. The earth was like a vast garden, surrounded by a magical river that flowed in both directions. On one side, it flowed to the west, on the other, it flowed to the east. And this place was so beautiful that it was called *Firdous*, or paradise. And you know, from what I've heard, it wasn't very far from here. It was on the seashore, very near the city of Akka. Today there is still a small village that goes by that name, paradise, and they say that the inhabitants of that village are all descendants of the Djenoune. Whether that is the truth, or a lie, I can't really say. In any case, eternal spring reigned in that garden, it was filled with flowers and fruits, fountains that never ran dry, and the inhabitants were never in want of food. They lived on fruit, honey, and herbs, for they did not know the taste of flesh. In the middle of the vast garden there was a magnificent cloud-colored palace, and the Djenoune lived in that palace, because they were the masters of the land, God had entrusted it to them. In those days, the Djenoune were kind, they never tried to harm anyone. Men, women and children lived in the garden around the palace. The air was so balmy, the sun so clement, that they had no need of houses to protect themselves, and winter never came and it was never cold. And now children, I am going to tell you how it was all lost. For the place where that garden once stood, the land so sweetly named Firdous, paradise, the garden filled with flowers and trees, where fountains and birds sang endlessly, the garden where human beings lived in peace and ate nothing but fruit and honey, is now the dry earth, the rough bare earth, with not a tree, not a flower, and humans in that land have become so vicious that they wage a ruthless and cruel war, abandoned by the Djenoune.

Aamma Houriya stopped talking. We remained very still, waiting for the rest of the story. It was while she was telling that story, I recall, that the young Baddawi, Saadi Abou Talib, came into the camp for the first time. He squatted down on his heels, a little off to one side, to listen to what our aunt was telling us. On that day Aamma Houriya was silent for a long time, so that we could hear our hearts beating, the soft sounds coming from other houses before nightfall, the babbling of babies, the barking of dogs. She knew the value of silence.

She went on: "You know, it was the water that was the most beautiful thing in that garden. It was like nothing you've ever seen, or tasted, or dreamt of, such clear water, so cool and pure that those who drank of it enjoyed eternal youth, they never grew old, they never died. Streams ran through the garden, winding their way to the wide river that flowed around the garden in both directions, from west to east and from east to west. That's what the world was like in those days. And it would still be like that, and we too would be in that garden today, in the shade of the trees—right now as I speak to you—listening to the music of fountains and the song of birds if it hadn't been that the Djenoune, the masters of the land, got angry at the humans and dried up all the springs, and poured salt in the wide river that turned into what it is today, an endless, bitter expanse."

Houriya paused again for a moment. We watched the sky growing slowly darker. Wisps of smoke twirled up here and there between the roofs of the shacks, but they were deceptive and illusory, we knew that. The old women had lit fires to boil some water, but they had nothing but a few herbs to throw into it, and a few roots that they'd pulled up in the hills. Some had nothing at all to cook, but they lit a fire out of habit, as if they could feed themselves on smoke like the spirits in the stories that Aamma Houriya told us. She continued her tale, and all of a sudden my heart started beating faster because I realized that it was really our story she was telling, the garden, the paradise that we had lost when the Djenoune had punished us with their anger.

"Why did the Djenoune get angry with the humans, why did they destroy the garden where we could have continued to live in eternal spring? Some say that it is because of a woman, because she wanted to enter the palace of the Djenoune, and to do so, she made the humans believe that they were as powerful as the Djenoune, and that they could easily throw them out of the palace, since they were more numerous. Others say that it was because of two brothers, one was named Souad and the other Safi. They were born of the same father, but of different mothers, and because of this they hated each other. Each son wanted to have the part of the garden that belonged to the other. They say that even as young children they fought each other with their bare hands and the Djenoune laughed at them scuffling like two young rams tumbling around in the dust. Then they grew older and they fought with sticks and stones, and the

Djenoune continued to laugh and make fun of them from up on the walls of their palace, near the clouds, saying they were like monkeys. But they became adults and the battle continued; now they used swords and rifles. The two men were equally strong and cunning. They inflicted cruel wounds on one another, their blood ran on the ground, but neither would admit he was beaten. The Djenoune still watched them from up on the walls of their palace, and they said, "Let them fight and exhaust their strength, then they can become friends." But that is when an old woman intervened, they say she was a witch with a black face, dressed in rags, and it might well have been Aïsha, because she was very old, and she knew all the secrets of the Djenoune. One after the other, the two brothers went to consult her, they promised her piles of gold if she would assure their victory. The old slave rummaged through her bags and gave each of them a present. To Souad, the elder, she gave a small cage which held a wild red beast that shone curiously in the night, and no one had ever seen anything like it in that garden. To the second young man, whose name was Safi, she gave a large leather bag that held an invisible and powerful cloud. For in those days, neither fire nor wind existed in the garden. So the two brothers, who were at the height of their enmity, threw their evil presents at one another, without giving it a thought. When the man with the small cage opened it, the wild red beast bounded out and immediately engulfed the trees and grasses and became immense. Then the other brother opened his leather bag and the wind came roaring out upon the raging flames and changed them into a gigantic wildfire that set the whole garden ablaze. The red flames burned everything up, the trees, the birds, and all the humans who were in the garden except for a few who found refuge in the wide river. Then, from their palace surrounded with black smoke, the Djenoune were no longer laughing. They said, "May God's curse be upon all mankind, and its future generations." And they left the devastated garden forever. And before they left they dried up all the springs and all the fountains, to be sure that nothing would grow upon that land; then they flung down a huge mountain of salt that shattered and spilled into the river. That is how the garden of *Firdous* became this arid desert and the wide river that ran around the garden became bitter and stopped flowing in both directions. And that's the end of my story. Since that day, the Djenoune have hated human beings and they have still not forgiven them, and Aïsha, the immortal slave woman, continues to roam this land, giving arms and death to those who listen to her words. God forbid that she should ever cross our path, children."

Night had fallen, Aamma Houriya stood up and walked over to the well to say her prayers, and each of the children returned to his own house. Stretched out in my place on the floor next to the door, I could still hear Aamma Houriya's voice, as light and even as her breathing. I smelled the odor of smoke in the sky, the odor of hunger, and I thought: how long will mankind be abandoned by the Djenoune?

Roumiya arrived at the Nour Chams Camp at the end of summer. She was already more than six months pregnant when she came. She was a very young woman, nearly a girl, with a very white face lined with fatigue, but there was still something childlike about her face, something that was accentuated by her blonde hair pulled into two even braids and her cool water-colored eyes that looked at you with a kind of frightened innocence, the way certain animals do. Aamma Houriya had immediately taken the girl under her wing. She brought her over to our house and moved her into the spot left by the old woman who had found shelter elsewhere. Roumiya was one of the Deir Yassin survivors. Roumiya's husband had been killed there, just as her mother and father had been, and her parents-in-law too. The foreign soldiers found her wandering around on the road and took her to a military hospital because they thought she was mad. As a matter of fact, maybe Roumiya really had gone mad, because ever since that day she'd taken to sitting for hours in a corner, not moving, not saying a word. The soldiers took her around to the camps near Jerusalem, to Jalazoun, to Mousakar, to Deir Ammar, then to Tulkarm, to Balata. And that is how she ended up coming to the end of the road, all the way out to our camp.

When she first came to our place, she didn't want to take her veil off, even in the house. She would sit near the doorway, absolutely still, wrapped in her long, dust-covered veil that reached down to her knees, and stare out with blank eyes. The children who lived around us said she was crazy, and when they walked past the door, or met her on the path near the entrance to the camp, they blew a little dust out of the hollow of their hand to ward off the evil spirits.

They spoke of her in whispers, saying *"habla, habla,"* she's gone mad, and they also said *"khayfi,"* she's been frightened, because her eyes were fixed and dilated like the eyes of a startled animal, but in truth, it was the children who were afraid. We always thought of her a bit like that, khayfi. But Aamma Houriya knew how to get through to her. She tamed Roumiya bit by bit each day. In the beginning, she brought her a bowl of porridge with Klim milk, just as she would for a child, and she ran her finger, moistened with saliva, over the girl's dry lips to make her start eating. She spoke to her gently, caressed her, and little by little Roumiya awakened, came back to life. I can remember the first time she took her veil off, her white face shone out in the light, her delicate nose, her childish mouth, the blue tattoo-marks on her cheeks and on her chin, and especially her hair, long, thick, full of copper and gold highlights. Never had I seen hair so lovely, and I understood why they'd given her that name, Roumiya, for she was not of our race.

For a brief moment, fear stopped shining in her eyes. She looked at us, at Aamma Houriya and me, but she didn't say anything, didn't smile. She hardly ever spoke, just a few words, to ask for some water or some bread, or else she would suddenly spout off a sentence that she didn't understand, and that didn't make any sense to us either.

At times I would get fed up with her, with her blank stare, and I'd go up on the rocky hill, up where Old Nas was buried, up where the Baddawi now lived in a hut he had built out of branches and stones. I stood over with the other children, as though I were looking for the supply trucks to come. Maybe it was Roumiya's beauty that drove me away, her silent beauty, her eyes that seemed to be looking through everything and draining it of all meaning.

When the sun climbed toward the highest point in the sky, and the walls of our house threw off heat like the walls of a furnace, Aamma Houriya bathed Roumiya's body with a towel soaked in water. Every morning, she went to fetch water at the well, because water was scarce and all mud-colored, and it needed to be left standing for a long time. It was her cooking and drinking ration, and Aamma Houriya used it to wash the young woman's belly, but no one else knew anything about it. Aamma Houriya said that the unborn child shouldn't be deprived of water, for he already lived, he could hear the sound of water running over the skin, he could feel its freshness, like rain. Aamma Houriya had strange ideas; it was like the stories she told, once you understood them, everything seemed so much clearer, so much more real.

When the sun reached the highest point in the sky and nothing stirred in the camp, with the heat encompassing the rough board and tarpaper shacks like flames in a furnace, Aamma Houriya hung her veil up in the doorway and it made a blue shade. Docilely, Roumiya allowed herself to be completely undressed. She was waiting for the water that came trickling down from the towel. Aamma Houriya's nimble fingers washed each part of her body, the nape of her neck, her shoulders, the small of her back. Her long braids twirled around on her back like wet snakes. And then Roumiya stretched out on her back and Aamma let the water run down over her breasts, onto her dilated stomach. At first I would leave, take a walk outside to avoid seeing all of that, I'd go teetering around in the blinding light. Afterwards, I stayed, almost in spite of myself, because there was something powerful, something incomprehensible and real, in the gestures of the old woman, like a slow ceremony, a prayer. Roumiya's enormous belly bulged up below the dark dress rolled up under her chin, just like a moon, white, streaked with pink in the blue half-light. Aamma's hands were strong, they twisted the towel over her skin, and the water tumbled down, making its secret sound in the cave-like house. I watched the young woman, I saw her belly, her breasts, her head thrown back with closed eyes, and I felt sweat running down my forehead, my back, making my hair stick to my cheeks. In our house, like a secret hidden amid the heat and drought outdoors, all I could hear was the sound of water trickling onto Roumiya's skin, her slow breathing and Aamma Houriya's voice humming a wordless lullaby, just a faint murmuring, a drawn out droning sound that she interrupted each time she dipped the towel into the bucket.

It all lasted an eternity, such a long time that when Aamma Houriya finished bathing Roumiya, the girl had fallen asleep under the veils darkening in spots on her damp belly.

Outside the sun was still dazzling. The camp was heavy with dust, with silence. Before nightfall, I was up on top of the hill, my ears filled with the sounds of water and the droning voice of the old woman. Perhaps I had stopped seeing the camp through the same eyes. It was as if everything had changed, as if I had just arrived, as if I were unfamiliar with the stones, the dark houses, the horizon obstructed by the hills, the dried-up valley scattered with scorched trees where the sea never comes.

We've been prisoners in this camp for such a long time. It's difficult for me to recall what it was like before, in Akka. The sea, the smell of the sea, the cry of the gulls. The fishing boats slipping across the bay at dawn. The call to prayer at dusk, in the twilight, as I walked through the olive groves by the ramparts. Birds flew up, lazy turtledoves, silver-winged pigeons suddenly crossing the sky, turning, tilting up, flying off in the opposite direction. In the gardens, the blackbirds twittered anxiously as night approached. I've lost all of that now.

Here, night comes swiftly, there is no call, no prayer, no birds. The blank sky changes color, reddens, and then the night rises from the depths of the ravines. In the spring, when I first arrived, nights were hot. The heat of the sun blew down from the rocky hills late into the night. Now it is autumn, nights are cold. No sooner does the sun disappear behind the hills than you feel a chill rising from the earth. People cover themselves as best they can, with the blankets that the United Nations distributed, with dirty cloaks, with sheets. Wood has become so scarce that we don't light fires at night anymore. Everything is dark, silent, freezing. We've been abandoned, far from the world, far from all life. I've never felt like this before. Very quickly, stars appear in the sky, making their beautiful patterns. I can remember long ago, I was walking on the beach with my father, and the patterns that the stars made seemed familiar to me. They were like the lights of unexplored cities hanging in the sky. Now their pale, cold light makes our camp seem even darker, even more abandoned. On nights when the moon is round, the stray dogs bark. "Death is passing," says Aamma Houriya. In the morning, the men take the bodies of dogs that have died in the night and throw them far from the camp.

Children also cry in the night. I feel a shudder running all through my body. When morning comes, shall they go looking for the bodies of children who have died in the night?

The Baddawi, the one they call Saadi, went to live up on the rocky hill near the place where old Nas is buried over a year ago now. Not far from the grave he built a shelter from old branches and a piece of canvas. He stays up there all day and all night long, almost without moving, staring at the road to Tulkarm. The children go up to see him every morning and together they keep watch on the road by which the supply truck will be arriving. But when the truck comes, he doesn't go down. He sits up there by his shelter, as though it were none of his concern. He never comes to get his share. Sometimes he's so hungry that he comes halfway down the hill and since our house is the first one he finds, he just stands there a few feet away. Aamma Houriya takes a little bread or a chickpea cake of her own making, she lays it on a stone, and then goes back into her house. Saadi approaches, his eyes fixed steadily on mine with a kind of hardened timidity that makes my heart race. The dogs roaming about in the hills around the camp have that same cast to their eyes. The Baddawi is the only one who isn't afraid of the dogs. Up there on the hill he speaks to them. That's what the children say, and when Aamma Houriya heard that, she said he was simple-minded and that was why our camp was protected.

Every morning, I went up to the top of the hill to watch

the United Nations truck arrive. That's what I'd say. But it was also to see the Baddawi sitting on the stone in front of his hut of branches, wrapped in his woolen cloak. His hair was long and unkempt, but he had the face of a young, still-beardless boy, with just a thin mustache. When I walked up to him, he looked at me, and I saw the color of his eyes, the same as those of stray dogs. He only came down from the hill to drink at the well. He waited in line, and when his turn came, he dipped the water out of the bucket with his hand, and he drank nothing more until evening. The girls made fun of him, but they were a little frightened of him too. They said that he hid in the bushes to spy on them when they went to urinate. They said that he tried to drag one girl off, and that she bit him. But that's just a lot of gossip.

Sometimes, when Aamma Houriya told a Djinn story, he came to listen. He didn't sit with the children. He sat a little apart, his head bent down toward the ground, listening. Aamma Houriya said that he's alone in the world, that he hasn't any family left. But no one knows where he's from, or how he happened to come out here to the end of the road, to Nour Chams. Perhaps he was here before everyone else, with a herd of goats, and he just stayed on when his animals died, not knowing where else to go. Maybe he was born here.

He came up to me, talked to me. He spoke in a gentle voice, with an accent I'd never heard before. Aamma Houriya said that he speaks like the people of the desert, like a Baddawi. That's why we call him that. He looked at me with his yellow eyes. He asked me who I was, where I came from. When I spoke to him of Akka and of the sea, he wanted to know what the sea was like. He'd never seen it. All he had ever seen was the great salt lake, and the immense valley of Ghor, and al-Moujib, where he said the palaces of the Djenoune were. And then I told him about what I had seen, the steady waves that come to die breaking against the walls of the city, the trees washed up on the beach, and at dawn, the sailboats slipping through the mist amid the flapping flight of pelicans. The smell of the sea, the taste of salt, the wind, the sun sinking into the sea every evening, right up to its very last spark. I loved the way he listened, his arms crossed over his cloak, his bare feet planted squarely on the ground.

I didn't talk the way Aamma Houriya did, because I didn't know any tales. I could only talk about what I'd seen. And he in turn spoke of what he knew, the mountains where he kept the herds near the great salt lake, walking day after day along the underground rivers that run beneath the sand, gnawing at herbs and bushes, with the dogs running out ahead of him as his sole companions, the nomad campsites, the smell of fires burning, women's voices, his brothers from afar with other herds meeting there, and then striking out again.

When I spoke to him, or when he spoke to me, children came to listen. Their eyes were wide with fever, their hair all matted, their dark skin shone through the rags of their clothing. But we were just like them, I, the girl from the city by the sea, and he, the Baddawi; nothing set us apart anymore, we all had the same stray-dog eyes. We talked every evening when twilight soothed the scorch of day, watching the thin wisps of smoke floating up from the camp, and then nothing seemed hopeless anymore. We could get away, be free again.

After that I didn't go to wait for the supply truck anymore, either. Up on top of the hill, sitting by Saadi, I saw the cloud of dust far away on the Tulkarm road, and I heard the riotous cries of the children chanting: "Flour!... Milk!...Flour!"

So Aamma Houriya had to go down for our rations. And I just sat there listening to Saadi, trying to remember even more about what it was like, long ago, on the beach in Akka when I waited for the fishing boats to come in, and tried to catch sight of my father's boat first.

Aamma scolded me: "The Baddawi has put a spell on you! I'll take a stick to him!" She was making fun of me.

The war is so far away. Nothing ever happens. At first the children played with pieces of wood, imitating the sounds of rifle shots, or else they threw stones, lying flat on the ground, as if they were grenades. Now they don't even do that anymore. They've forgotten how. "Why don't we leave this place? Why don't we go back home?" They used to ask that too, and now they can't remember. Their mothers and fathers avert their faces.

There is a kind of film clouding the men's eyes. It makes them look foggy, their gaze is shallow, unrecognizable. There's no more hatred, no anger, no more tears, or desire, or restlessness. Maybe it's because water is so very scarce, water, the sweet side of life. And so there is this milky film, just as in the eyes of the white she-dog when it started to die. That's why I love Saadi's eyes. The water hasn't gone out of his eyes. His yellow irises shine out like those of the dogs roaming about in the hills around the camp. He's laughing, but to himself, without moving his lips, with his eyes only. It's very plain to see.

Sometimes he talks about the war. He says that when it's all over, he'll go south, down by the great salt lake, to the valley of his birth. He'll go in search of his father, his brothers, his uncles and his aunts. He thinks that he'll find them and that one day he can go back to walking with the herd along the invisible rivers again.

He says names that I've never heard before, names as distant as stars: Suweima, Suweili, Basha, Safut, Madasa, Kamak, and Wadi al-Sirr, the river of the secret, where everyone goes in the end. Out there, according to him, the land is so harsh, and the wind so strong, that men are swept along like bits of dust. When the wind rises, the herd walks toward the River Jordan, and sometimes even beyond, all the way to the great city of al-Quds, the one the Hebrews call Jerusalem. When the wind dies down, the herd returns to the desert. He says, just the way old Nas did: Does the land not belong to everyone? Does the sun not shine for us all? His face is young, but his eyes are very knowing. He isn't a prisoner at the Nour Chams camp. He can go whenever he likes, cross the hills, go to those golden and pearl-colored cities where Aamma Houriya says kings once lived who ruled even the Djenoune, to Baghdad, to Isfahan, to Basra.

One night I was so sick I was burning up inside. It felt as if a stone were lying on my chest. I left the shack. Outside everything was calm. Aamma Houriya was sleeping wrapped up in her sheet by the door, but Roumiya wasn't asleep. Her eyes were wide open. I could see her chest rising and falling as she breathed but she didn't say anything when I went past her.

I saw the stars. Little by little everything started shining brightly in the dark, shining with a hard, painful light. The air was hot, the wind seemed to come blowing down from the mouth of an oven. Yet no one was outside. Even the dogs were hiding.

I looked at the straight lines of the alleys in the camp, the tarred roofs of the houses, the pieces of sheet metal rattling in the wind. It was as if everyone were dead, as if everything had disappeared, forever. I don't know why I did it: suddenly, I was afraid, I was in so much pain because of the weight on my chest, because of the fever that was burning inside of me, all the way down to the bone. So I started running down the alleys of the camp, not knowing where I was going, and shouting: "Wake up! Wake up!" At first my voice wouldn't come out of my throat, I only let out a hoarse cry that ripped through me, a crazed cry. It echoed out oddly in the sleepy camp and soon the dogs started barking, one, then another, then all the dogs around the camp and all the way up into the invisible hills. And I just kept running down the alleys, barefoot in the dust, with that burning feeling in my throat and in my body, the pain that didn't want to loosen its grip. I shouted to everyone, to all the plank-and-sheet-metal houses, to all the tents, to all the cardboard shacks: "Wake up! Wake up!" People started coming out. Men appeared, women draped in their coats despite the heat. I was running and could distinctly hear what they were saying, the same thing they'd said when Roumiya arrived: "She's crazy, she's gone crazy." The children woke up, the older ones ran along with me, the others were crying in the dark. But I couldn't stop anymore. I ran and ran through the camp, going through the same streets time and again, first over by the hill, then down toward the wells, and along the barbed wire fencing that the foreigners had put around the wells and I could hear my breath wheezing in my lungs, I could hear my heart pounding, I could feel the heat of the sun on my face, on my chest. I was shouting in a voice that was no longer my own: "Wake up! Prepare yourselves!"

Then all of a sudden I couldn't catch my breath. I fell to the ground near the barbed wire. I couldn't move anymore, couldn't speak. The people walked up to me, women, children. I could hear the sound of their footsteps, I could clearly hear their breathing, their words. Someone brought some water in a metal goblet, the water ran into my mouth, over my cheek, like blood. I made out Aamma's face, very near to me. I pronounced her name. She was there, her soft hand lying on my forehead. She was murmuring words that I didn't understand. Then I realized they were prayers and I felt the Djenoune moving away from me, abandoning me. Suddenly, I felt empty, terribly weak.

I was able to walk, leaning on Aamma's arm. Stretched out on the mat in our house, I heard the sound of the voices fading away. The dogs kept barking for a long time and I fell asleep before they did.

When I went up to the top of the rocky hill in the morning, Saadi came up to me and said, "Come on, I want to talk to you." It was still early, there weren't any children out yet. I noticed that Saadi had changed. He'd washed his face and hands down at the wells at prayer time, and even though his clothes were torn, they were clean. He held my hand very tightly in his and his eyes were filled with a brightness I had never seen. He said, "Nejma, I heard your voice last night. I wasn't sleeping when you started calling to us. I realized you had received the message from God. No one heard you, but I heard your call and that's why I have prepared myself."

I wanted to pull my hand away and leave, but he was holding it so fast that I couldn't escape. The hill was deserted, silent, the camp was far away. I was afraid, and the fear was mingling with a feeling I didn't understand. He said, "I want you to come with me. We're going to cross the river, till we reach the valley of my birth, al-Moujib. You'll be my wife and we will have sons, God willing." He was speaking without haste and a sort of joy lit his eyes. That's what attracted and frightened me at the same time. "If you like we can even leave today. We'll take some bread, a little water, and we'll cross the mountains." He was pointing eastward, toward the hills still in darkness.

The sky was blank, the sun was beginning its ascent. The earth was shining with new freshness. Below, at the bottom of the hill, stood the camp like a dark smear from which a few trails of smoke arose. You could see the shapes of women near the wells, children running in the dust.

"Talk to me Nejma. All you have to do is say yes and we'll go today. No one can keep us here." I said, "It can't be, Saadi. I can't go away with you." His eyes darkened, he let go of my hand and sat down on a rock. I sat next to him. I could hear my heart beating hard in my chest, because I wanted to go. I began to talk so I could stop listening to my heart. I talked about Aamma Houriya, about Roumiya and the child that was going to be born. I talked about my city, Akka, to which I had to return. He listened without responding, looking out at the vast valley, the camp, so like a prison with those people coming and going along the alleys like ants, busying themselves around the wells. He said, "I thought I'd understood your call, the call that God sent you last night." He said that in a calm voice, but he was sad and I felt tears in my eyes, and my heart started racing again because I wanted to go away. Now I took his hands in mine, his fingers that were so very long and thin and the pale marks of his nails against his black skin. I felt the blood running through his hands. "Maybe one day I'll go away, Saadi. But I can't leave now. Are you angry with me?" He looked at me, smiling, and his eyes were bright again. "So that was the message that God sent you? Then I will stay too."

We walked a little ways on the hilltop. When we came up in front of his shelter, I saw he'd prepared a bundle for the road. Food wrapped in a piece of cloth and a bottle of water attached with a string. "When the war is over, I'll take you to our house, in Akka. There are lots of fountains there, we won't need to take water with us."

He unwrapped the bundle and we sat down on the ground to eat a little bread. The sunlight was burning off the morning freshness. We heard the bustling of the camp, the children who were coming up. There was even the swift flight of a bird, letting out sharp cries. We both burst out laughing because it had been so long since we'd seen a bird. I laid my head on Saadi's shoulder. I listened to his halting, melodious voice speaking about the valley where he followed the flock with his brothers along the underground river of al-Moujib.

After that came the winter and life became difficult in Nour Chams. We had been in the camp for almost two years now. The supply truck came less and less frequently, twice a week, or even only once. A whole week went by without the truck coming to the camp. There were rumors of war, people said terrible things. They said that in Al-Quds, the old part of the city had burned down and that the Arab soldiers threw burning tires into the cellars and the stores. Refugees came in the truck, men, women, children with distraught faces. They weren't poor peasants anymore as in the beginning. They were richer people from Haifa, Jaffa, shopkeepers, lawyers, even a dentist. When they climbed out of the truck the ragged children from the camp swarmed around them, chanting, "Foulous! Foulous!" They followed the newcomers until they gave up a few coins. But the new refugees didn't know where to go in the camp. Some slept out in the open with their suitcases piled up at their feet, wrapped in their blankets. For them, the truck had brought cigarettes, tea, Marie biscuits. The truck drivers sold it all to them in secret, while the poor people were waiting in line to get their rations of flour, Klim milk, dried meat.

When the newcomers got out of the truck, people gathered around, asked them questions. "Where are you from? What news have you brought? Is it true that Jerusalem is burning? Does anyone know my father, old Serays, who lives on the road to Aïn Karim? You, did you happen to see my brother? He lives in the largest house in Suleïman, the one with a furniture store? What about my drapery store, facing the Gate of Damas, was it spared? And my pottery store near the Omar Mosque? And what's become of my house in al-Aksa, a lovely white house with two palm trees in front of the door, Mehdi Abu Tarash's house? Have you heard anything about my neighborhood, near the train station? Is it true that the English bombed it?" The newcomers advanced through the questions, dazed by the journey, blinking their eyes because of the dust, their fine clothes already stained with sweat, and gradually the questions stopped, silence returned. The inhabitants of the camp fell away as they passed, still trying to read an answer to their questions in the blank eyes, the slumped shoulders, in the children's faces glistening with fear like a feverish sweat.

That was when the first city-dwellers arrived, fleeing the bombs. Their money was worthless here. In vain, they had handed out bills by the fistful all along the road. To pay for a pass, for the right to stay just a little longer in their home, for a seat in the tarpaulined truck that brought them to the camp at the end of the road.

Then the rations got even skimpier because of all the people who had come into the camp. Death struck everywhere now. When I went to the wells in the morning, the passageway between the barbed wire fences was scattered with the cadavers of dogs. Those still alive, growling like wild beasts, fought over the remains. The children could no longer wander far from the houses for fear of being devoured by the dogs. When I went up to the top of the stone hill to see Saadi, I had to carry a stick to ward off the dogs. He wasn't afraid. He wanted to stay up there. His eyes were still bright and he took me by the hand to talk with me and his voice was gentle. But I didn't stay very long anymore. Roumiya was on the verge of giving birth and I didn't want to be far from her when it happened.

Aamma Houriya was worn out. She couldn't bathe Roumiya any longer. Now the wells were almost dry, in spite of the rains. Those who were last to throw their bucket in brought up only mud. You had to wait all night for the water to reappear at the bottom of the wells.

The only food was oatmeal mixed with Klim milk. The able-bodied men, the young boys of ten or twelve, and even the women, left one after another. They went northward toward Lebanon, or eastward in the direction of Jordan. People said they were going to join the Fedayeen, the martyrs. They were called the *aïdoune*, the revenants, because one day they would return. Saadi didn't want to go to war, he didn't want to be a revenant. He was waiting for me to go away with him to the valley of his childhood, to al-Moujib, on the far side of the vast salt lake.

Roumiya hardly went out of the house anymore, only to go to the bathroom in the ravine outside the camp. She only went with me, or sometimes Aamma Houriya accompanied her as she teetered along the path holding her belly in her hands.

It was there, in the ravine that the pains started. I was up on top of the hill because it was early in the morning and the sun was very low, lighting the land through the mist. It was a time for the Djenoune, a time when the red flames might be dancing near the well in Zikhron Yaacov, as Aamma Houriya had seen just before the English came.

I heard a sharp cry, a cry that pierced the dawn silence. I left Saadi and started running down the hill, cutting my bare feet on the sharp stones. The cry had come only once and I stopped short, trying to guess where it had come from. When I entered our house I saw the sheets thrown to one side. The jar of water that I'd filled at daybreak was still full. Instinctively, I went toward the ravine. My heart was racing because the scream had lodged inside of me, I knew it was time, Roumiya was going to give birth. I ran through the brush toward the ravine. I heard her voice again. She wasn't screaming, she was moaning, groaning louder and louder, then stopping as if to catch her breath. When I went into the ravine, I saw her. She was lying on the ground with her knees up, wrapped in her blue veil, her head covered. Aamma Houriya was sitting next to her, caressing her, talking to her. The ravine was still in shadow. The night chill attenuated the smell of urine and excrement. Aamma Houriya lifted her head. For the first time I saw an expression of helplessness on her face. Her eyes were blurred with tears. She said, "We have to carry her. She can't walk." I was going to go for help but Roumiya pulled the veil from her face, she sat up. Her child's face was twisted with pain and anxiety. Her hair was damp with sweat. She said, "I want to stay here. Help me." Then the moans started again, punctuated by the contractions of her uterus. I just stood before her unable to move, unable to think. Aamma Houriya snapped at me, "Go get some water, the sheets!" And since I didn't move, "Hurry up! She's started labor." So I started running with the sound of my blood roaring in my ears and my breath whistling in my throat. In the house I took the sheets, the jar of water, and because I was in such a hurry, the water was slopping out of the jug and drenching my dress. The children were following me. When I got to the entrance of the ravine I told them to go away. But they stayed, they scaled the sides of the ravine to watch. I threw stones at them. They backed away, then they returned.

Roumiya was suffering a great deal, lying on the ground. I helped Aamma lift her up to wrap her in the sheet. Her dress was soaked from the waters and on her bloated white stomach the contractions looked like waves on the surface of the sea. I'd never seen that before. It was terrifying and beautiful at the same time. Roumiya wasn't at all the same, her face had changed. Thrown backwards, looking up at the bright sky, her face seemed like a mask, as if some other person were beneath it. Mouth open, Roumiya was panting. Now and again whimpering sounds that were no longer her voice rose from her throat. I ventured a little closer. With a dampened cloth I put water on her face. She opened her eyes, she looked at me as if she didn't recognize me. She murmured, "It hurts, it hurts." I wrung the cloth over her lips so she could drink.

The wave came back on her belly, went all the way up to her face. She arched her body backwards, pinched her lips closed as if to prevent her voice from coming out, but the wave was still swelling and the moan slipped out, became a scream, then broke, became a panting breath. Aamma Houriya had placed her hands on Roumiya's belly, and she pushed with all of her weight, as hard as if she were trying to push the dirt from a piece of laundry on the edge of the washtub. I looked on in terror, the grimacing face of the old woman as she mauled Roumiya's belly, I felt as though I were witnessing a crime.

Suddenly the wave started moving faster. Roumiya arched up high, heels dug into the sand, shoulders against the stones in the ravine, face turned toward the sun. With a supernatural scream she pushed the child out of her body, then slowly fell back to the ground. So now there was that shape, that being covered with blood and placenta wearing a living cord around its body, which Aamma Houriya had taken and started to wash and that suddenly let out its first cry.

I looked at Roumiya stretched out, her dress pulled up on her belly, bruised from Aamma's fists, her swollen breasts with purple tips. I felt nauseated, profoundly dizzy. When Aamma Houriya finished washing the baby, she cut the cord with a stone, knotted the wound on the child's belly. For the first time she looked at me with a peaceful face. She showed me the baby, tiny, wrinkled, "It's a girl! A very pretty girl!" She said that in a relaxed voice as if she'd found the baby in a basket. She laid it down gently on its mother's breast where milk was already dribbling out. Then she covered them with a clean sheet and sat down next to them humming. Now the sun was rising in the sky. The women began to come into the ravine. The men and the children kept their distance on the slopes of the ravine. The flies whirled overhead. Aamma Houriya seemed to suddenly remember the horrid smell. "We'd better be getting home." Some women brought a blanket. Five of them together lifted Roumiya holding her baby tightly to her breast, and they carried her away slowly like a princess.

Life had changed now that the baby was in our house. Despite the lack of food and water there was new hope for us. Even the neighbors felt it. Every morning they came to our door, they brought a present, sugar, clean linen, a little powdered milk they'd taken from their rations. The old women who had nothing to offer brought dead branches for the fire, roots, fragrant herbs.

Roumiya had changed too since the birth of the baby. She no longer had that foreign look in her eyes, she stopped hiding behind her veil. She'd given her daughter the name of Loula because it was the first time. Al-marra al-loula. And I thought it was true—here in our miserable camp where the world had cast us, far from everything. Now there was a heart in the camp, there was a center, and it was in our house.

Aamma Houriya never tired of telling all the women who came to visit about the birth, as if it were a miracle. She said, "Just think, I took Roumiya to the ravine so she could go to the bathroom just before sunrise. And God willed that the child be born there in that ravine, as if to show that the most beautiful thing can appear in the most vile place, amidst the refuse." She elaborated upon that theme infinitely, and it became a legend that the women spread around through the grapevine. The women stuck their heads into the house, holding their veils in place, to get a glimpse of the wondrous thing, Roumiya sitting down giving her milk to Loula. And it was true, the legend that Aamma Houriya had invented enveloped her in a special kind of light, with her clean white dress, her long blond hair hanging over her shoulders, and that baby sucking at her breast. Something was truly going to begin, it was the first time.

It was in winter when our camp became desperate, hungry, abandoned. The children and the old men were dying from fever and illnesses caused by the well water. It was mostly in the lower part of the camp where the newcomers had settled. Saadi could see the people burying the dead from up on the hill. There were no coffins, the bodies were wrapped in old sheets, without even sewing them up, and holes were hurriedly dug on the side of the hill with a few big rocks on top to keep the stray dogs from digging them up. But we wanted to think that it was all happening far away and that, thanks to Loula, nothing like that could happen to us.

It was cold now. At night the wind blew over the stony land, burned your eyelids, numbed your limbs. Sometimes it rained and I listened to the sound of the water running over the planks and tarpaper. In spite of our hardships, to me it seemed as fine as if we were in a house with nice high dry walls and a pool in the courtyard where the rain would be making its music. To catch the rain, Aamma put all the receptacles she could find under the rainspouts—pots, jars, empty powdered milk cans, and even an old car hood that the children found in the riverbed. So I listened to the rain tinkling in all the receptacles and I was feeling as joyful as I did in the old days, in my house, when I listened to the water cascading down over the roof and onto the tiles of the courtyard, and watering the orange trees in pots that my father had planted. It was a sound that made me feel like crying too, because it spoke to me, it told me that nothing would ever again be the way it was before, and that I would never see my home again, or my father, or the neighbors, or anything I used to know.

Aamma Houriya came to sit down beside me as if she sensed my sadness. She spoke to me gently, maybe she told me a Djinn story, and I leaned against her, but without letting myself be too heavy because she was weak from all the privations. Earlier in the evening when the rain had started falling she had joked, "Now this old plant will turn green again." But I knew that the rain wouldn't bring back her strength. She was so pale and thin, and she coughed constantly.

Now it was Roumiya who took care of her. Aamma looked after the baby wrapped in cloths, she sang it lullabies.

The United Nations truck hadn't been back for a long time. The children went into the hills looking for roots, leaves, and myrtle fruit to eat. Saadi knew the desert well. He knew how to trap prey, small birds and jerboas that he roasted and shared with us. I never would have thought I could take so much pleasure in eating such tiny creatures. He also brought back wild berries, arbutus, that he gathered far away, beyond the hills. When he brought his harvest tied in a scrap of cloth that he laid ceremoniously on the flat rock in front of the door, we pounced on the fruit to eat and suck them avidly and he teased us in a placating voice, "Don't bite your fingers. Don't eat the rocks."

Something strange was going on between the Badawi and Roumiya. She, who used to look away when Saadi came near the house, now pulled her veil over her face as if to hide but her clear eyes stared at the young man. In the morning when I came back from the wells I didn't have to go up on the hill to find Saadi. He was there, sitting on the flat rock next to the house. He didn't speak to anyone, he stayed a little off to one side, as if he were waiting for someone. Now I couldn't take his hand in mine anymore, or put my head on his shoulder to listen to him. He spoke to me with the same soft and melodious voice, but I knew it was no longer me he was waiting for. It was Roumiya's silhouette hidden in the shadow of the house, Roumiya and her long hair through which Aamma Houriya was running a fine comb, Roumiya who was breast-feeding her baby, or who was fixing the meal with flour and oil. At times they talked to each other. Roumiya sat on the doorstep, wrapped in her blue veil, and Saadi sat on the other side of the door and they talked, they laughed.

So then I'd go up on top of the hill, carrying my stick to ward off the dogs. There were no more children up there, I kept a lookout for the supply truck by myself. The sunlight was blinding, the wind blew up clouds of dust in the valley. In the distance the horizon was gray, blue, intangible. I could imagine I was by the sea, on the beach in the dusk and I was watching for the fishing boats, to be the first to see the one I knew so well, with its red sail and, on its keel, the green star of my name that accompanied my father.

One morning a stranger came into our camp escorted by soldiers. I was up on the hilltop standing watch when the large cloud of dust rose on the road to Zeïta, and I realized it wasn't the food trucks. My heart started pounding with fear because I thought they were soldiers coming to kill us.

When the convoy came into the camp everyone was hiding because they were afraid. Then the men came out of the cabins and the women and children came with them. I ran down the hill.

The trucks and the cars stopped at the entrance to the

camp and some men and women got out, soldiers, doctors, nurses. Some were taking pictures or talking with the men, handing out candy to the children.

I moved up through the crowd to hear what they were saying. The men in white spoke in English and I only caught one or two words that I understood. "What are they saying?" a woman asked worriedly. In her arms was a child with an emaciated face, its head balding with ringworm. "They are doctors, they've come to treat the sick." I said that to reassure her. But she kept watching them, her face half-hidden behind her veil, and repeated, "What are they saying?"

Among the soldiers was a very tall, slender, elegant foreigner dressed in gray. While all the others were wearing helmets, he was bareheaded. He had a gentle, slightly red face, he would lean his head to one side to listen to what the doctors were saying to him. I thought he was the boss of the foreigners and I inched closer to see him better. I wanted to go up to him, I wanted to talk to him, tell him all that we were suffering, the children who died here every night, whom we buried in the morning at the foot of the hill, the weeping of women that droned from one end of the camp to the other, so that you had to plug up your ears and run up the hill to keep from hearing them.

When they started walking through the streets with the soldiers my heart started beating very fast. I ran toward them shamelessly, despite my torn dress and tangled hair and my dirt-stained face. The soldiers didn't see me right away because they were keeping their eyes to the side in case someone wanted to attack them. But he, the tall man with light-colored clothes, saw me and stopped walking—his eyes fixed on me, as if he were questioning me. I could see his gentle face, reddened from the sun, his silver hair. The soldiers stopped me, held me back, they were squeezing my arms so hard it hurt. I realized I'd never reach the boss, that I wouldn't be able to talk to him, so I shouted the only words I knew in English, "Good morning, sir! Good morning, sir!" I was shouting that with all my might and I wanted him to understand with only those words what I wanted to tell him. But the soldiers pulled me away and the group of men in white and the nurses walked on. He, their boss, turned back toward me, he looked at me smiling, he said something I didn't understand but I think it was simply, "Good morning," and all the people walked on with him. I saw him walking away through the camp, his tall light-colored shape, his head tilted to one side. I went back to join the others, the women, the children. I was so tired from what I'd done that I didn't feel the pain in my arms, or even the bitter disappointment of not having been able to say anything.

I went back to our house. Aamma Houriya was lying under the blanket. I saw how pale and thin she was. She asked me if the food truck had finally come and, to comfort her, I told her that the truck had brought everything, bread, oil, milk, dried meat. I also told her about the doctors and nurses, the medicine. Aamma Houriya said, "That's good. That's good." She remained there, lying on the floor under the blanket, her head resting on a stone.

Sickness came to the camp in spite of the doctors' visit. Death was no longer furtive, carrying off old men and children in the night, a cold feeling that crept into the bodies of the weaker people and snuffed out the warmth of life. It was a plague that roamed the alleys of the camp sowing death in broad daylight, every minute, even among the most able-bodied men.

It had all started with the rats that we saw dying in the narrow streets of the camp right out in the sunlight as if they'd been chased from the ravines. At first the children played with the dead rats and the women picked them up with a stick and threw them a little further away. Aamma Houriya said that they should be burned, but there was no gasoline or wood to make a bonfire.

The rats had come from all sides. At night we could hear them running over the roofs of the houses, their claws made little screeching sounds on the sheet metal and the planks.

It was death they were fleeing. When I went out at dawn to fetch water for the day, the ground around the wells was strewn with dead rats. Even the stray dogs didn't touch them.

The children died first, those who had played with the dead rats. Word spread through the camp because children—the brothers or friends of those who died—ran through the camp shouting. Their shrill voices echoing the terrible, incredible words that even they didn't understand, like the names of demons, "*Habouba!...Kahoula!...*" The cries of the children reverberated like the cawing of sinister birds in the still afternoon air. I came out into the burning sun, I walked through the alleys of the camp. It was deserted. Everything seemed sleepy, yet death was everywhere. In the north end of the camp—where the newcomers were, the rich people from al-Quds, Jaffa, Haifa, who'd fled the war—some people were gathered in front of a house. One of the men was dressed like an Englishman, but his clothing was torn and soiled. He was the dentist from Haifa. He was the one who had welcomed the doctors and the boss of the foreigners into the camp. I'd seen him with the soldiers. He'd watched me when I'd run up to them to try and talk with the man in light-colored clothes.

He was standing in front of the house with a handkerchief over his face. Next to him, women were crying, collapsed on the ground, their veils over their mouths and noses. In the darkness of the house the body of a young boy was stretched out on the floor. The skin on his chest and stomach had dark blue marks on it and there were terrifying splotches on his face and all the way down to the palms of his hands.

The sun beat down in the cloudless sky, the rocky hills around the camp shimmered in the heat. I remember that I walked slowly through the streets, barefoot in the dust, listening to the sounds that came from the houses. I could hear my heart thumping and there was silence all around in that blinding light as if death had spread over the entire world. In the houses, people hid in the shadows. I couldn't hear their voices but I knew that here and there other women, men, were sick with the plague, and were burning with fever and moaning with pain because of the swollen, hard glands under their arms, in their neck, in their groin. I thought of Aamma Houriya and I was sure that the fatal marks had already appeared on her body. I felt nauseated. I couldn't go home. Despite the heat, I climbed the stony slope up to the top of the hill, all the way up to Old Nas's grave.

There were no more children up there, and the Baddawi wasn't in his shelter of branches. No one waited for the food truck to arrive anymore. The plague would wipe out every living person in Nour Chams. Perhaps it had even infected the whole earth, a scourge that the Djenoune sent to mankind, as God had commanded, so they would stop making war; and then when they were all dead and the sand of the desert had covered their bones, the Djenoune would come back, they would reign once again in their palace overlooking the garden of paradise.

I waited all day long in the shade of the scorched shrubs, hoping for I know not what. Hoping maybe that Saadi would come. But ever since he'd been living next to our house he windows, its spiked gates. I saw the shrunken olive tree that was planted in the park as a symbol of peace. I saw the sundial with its Latin inscription that made me think of expressions used in the Pickwick Club. I looked for the building in which my mother and father lived, with a balcony overlooking the river. But today the river has been filled in with parking lots and pretentious concrete constructions. Nearby, in an old building, is a hotel with a name that I love—Hôtel Soledad, Solitude Hotel. I took a little room on the courtyard side because of the noisy traffic. When I'm stretched out on the narrow bed, I can hear pigeons cooing, and the faint burbling of a radio, and children shouting. It seems to me that I might be anywhere, everywhere, nowhere.

So many days spent in this strange city, in the blazing forest fires. Every day brought the echoes of war in Lebanon and new fires that had broken out in the Maures, the Esterel, in the hills of the Var. Every day in the narrow hospital room faced with my mother's pallid and gaunt body, every day watching her fade a little more, disappear. I listened to her weak, distant voice, felt her hand in mine. She spoke of the old days, of my father. She said Michel, she spoke of Nice, Antibes, she spoke of happy days, walks along the shore, vacations in Italy, in Siena, Florence, Rome. She spoke to me about it all as if I'd been there, somewhere, already grown up, a friend, a sister, a young woman whom a couple meets by chance at a hotel, by a lake, and who shares an instant of their happiness, like an intrusion. The restaurant in Amantea, the sea so very blue, the headlands stretching out into the twilight. I'd been there with her, with my father, I had eaten the fresh watermelon, drunk the wine, heard the music of the waves and the cries of seagulls. Everything else disappeared then, when she spoke to me of Amantea, of days during the summer after their marriage, as if I'd been there too and I'd seen their faces lit with youth, heard their voices, their knowing laughter. She spoke, and her hand gripped mine very tightly, as she must have held my father's hand back then when they'd gone out on that boat, gliding over the sparkling sea, surrounded by the riotous cries of seagulls.

Elizabeth's voice was growing gradually fainter every day, she told the same story endlessly, repeated the same names, the same cities, Pisa, Rome, Naples, and always the name Amantea, as if it had been the only place in the world that war had never reached. Her voice was so weak in the last days that I had to lean all the way down to her lips, feel the breath that carried the words, the shreds of memories.

Every day leaving the hospital at dusk and walking aimlessly through the streets, my mind swimming, hearing that name repeated infinitely, until it became an obsession, Amantea, Amantea...Reading in the papers about the fires burning on all the mountains, devouring forests of holm oaks and pines in Toulon, in Fayence, in Draguignan, in the Tanneron Mountains. The fires that lit up Beirut as it lay dying.

So I walked through the scorched streets at night, searching for shadows, memories. And Elizabeth's hand gripping mine and her voice murmuring incomprehensible words, words of love that she uttered on the beach in Amantea, lying close against my father's body, the words that he said—like a secret—and the sea seemed even more beautiful, filled with sparks of light, each wave moving eternally toward the beach. In the last days she couldn't even speak anymore but the words were still in her, they came up to the edge of her lips and I leaned over to grasp them on her breath, to hear them once again, the words of life. I talked to her now since she was no longer able to, it was I who spoke to her of it all, of Siena, of Rome, of Naples, of Amantea, as if I'd been there, as if it had been I who had held my father's hand on the beach, watching the fitful flight of seagulls in the evening sky, listening to the music of the waves, watching the light fade beyond the sea rim. I pressed her hand and I spoke to her, watching her face, her chest barely lifting the sheet, holding her hand tightly to give her some of my strength. In the embattled city, there was no more water, no more bread, just the flickering light of the fires, the rumble of battle, and the silhouettes of children wandering through the ruins. It was the end of August, whole mountains were burning above Saint-Maxime.

At night as I walked through the hills after leaving the hospital, the sky was aglow as if with the setting sun. In the Var, seventeen thousand acres were in flames, there was a taste of ash in the air, in the water, even in the sea. Freighters sailed away from the ruined city carrying cargos of men. Their names had etched themselves in my memory, they were *Sol Georgios*, *Alkion*, *Sol Phryne*, *Nereus*. They were sailing for Cyprus, Aden, Tunis, Port Sudan. They moved over the smooth sea and the waves in their wakes would widen till they broke upon the shore, upon the beaches. The seagulls kept them company for a long time in the pale twilit sky until the buildings on shore faded to tiny white spots. In the maze of streets, faces questioned me, eyes watched me. I saw women, children slipping like shadows down the crumbling streets, the ruts of the refugee camps in Sabra, in Chatila. The boats sailed away, they were headed for the other side of the world, for the far side of the sea. The *Atlantis* slipped slowly along the wharf, it was moving out toward the glassy sea in the hot evening wind, it was as tall and white as a building. It was going north, toward Greece, toward Italy perhaps. I searched the sea, the ash-gray sea, as if I would see it appear in the dark dusk, its lights shining, gliding along in its wake, surrounded by the whirl of seagulls.

Elizabeth was so weak she couldn't see anymore. I spoke to her for a long time, very close to her ear, feeling the strands of gray hair against my lips. I tried to say the words she loved, the names, Naples, Florence, Amantea, because those were the words that could still penetrate her and mix with her blood, with her breath. The nurses had tried to keep me away but I remained, clinging to the bars of the bed, my head resting on the same pillow, I waited, I breathed, I lived. Water ran into her veins from the tube, drop after drop and the words were like those drops, they came one after the other, imperceptible, very low, very slow—the sun, the sea, the black rocks, the flight of birds, Amantea, Amantea...Medicines, injections, brutal and frightful treatments, and Elizabeth's hand suddenly clenching mine, strengthened by suffering. The words again, to gain time, to stay a little longer, to keep from parting. The sun, the fruit, the sparkling wine in the glasses, the streamlined shapes of tartans, the town of Amantea growing drowsy in the afternoon heat, the cool sheets under naked skin, the blue shade of closed shutters. I had known that too, I was there, with my father, with my mother, I was in the shadows, in the coolness, in the flesh of the fruit. War had never come there, nothing had ever troubled the immensity of the smooth sea.

Elizabeth died during the night. When I went into the room, I saw her body lying on the stretcher, wrapped in a sheet, her face very white, very thin, with the peaceful smile that didn't seem real. Both suffering and life had ended in her at the same time. I looked at her for a moment, then I left. I no longer felt anything. I filled out the necessary papers and a taxi took me to the crematorium for the sinister ritual. The oven heated to fifteen hundred degrees turned the person who had been my mother into a pile of ashes. Then, in exchange for money, I was given an iron cylinder with a screw-on lid that I put in my shoulder bag. I'd been in this city for years, it seemed to me I would never be able to leave.

Each day that followed I roamed the streets with my bag in the metallic heat of the fires around the city. I didn't know what I was looking for. Maybe the shadows the officers of the Gestapo tracked through this city, all of those they had condemned to death and who had hidden in cellars, in attics. Those whom the German army had captured in the Stura valley and locked up at the camp in Borgo San Dalmazzo near the train station, who left in armored boxcars, who came through the station in Nice during the night, who continued their journey northward, to Drancy, and farther still, to Dachau, to Auschwitz? I walked through the streets of this city, faces floated in front of me, lit by the glow of the streetlamps. Men leaned toward me, murmured words into my ear. Young people laughed, walking along with their arms around each other's waists. The people that Prefect Ribières had condemned to death, issuing an order of expulsion against them. On a beach across the sea, while the city seems to stand transfixed in its destruction, the women and children of the refugee camps watch the boats drifting away on the smooth sea. And here in this city people come and go in the streets past the brightly lit shop windows, they are indifferent, remote. They walk by corners where martyred children were hung by the neck from the moldings of streetlamps as if from butcher hooks.

The day after Elizabeth ended in the crematorium, I walked around on top of the hill in Cimiez, through streets gleaming with sunlight, filled with the smell of cypress, of pittospores. There were cats running between the cars, insolent blackbirds. On the roofs of the villas, turtledoves danced. The smell of the fires had disappeared now and there were no more clouds in the sky. I didn't know what I was looking for, what I wanted to see. It was like a wound in my heart, I wanted to see the evil, understand what had escaped me, what had cast me into another world. It seemed that if I could find a trace of that evil, I would at last be able to leave, forget, start my life over, with Michel, with Philip, the two men I love. At last I would again be able to travel, talk, discover places and faces, live in the present. I haven't much time. If I don't find where the evil is, I will have lost my life and my truth. I will continue to wander.

I walked around for so many days through the squares, my bag on my shoulder, past the luxury apartment buildings that look out over the sea. Then I came up in front of a large white building, so beautiful, so peaceful, lit with the last rays of the sun. That was what I'd wanted to see. Beautiful and sinister, like a royal palace, surrounded by its formal garden, its basin of calm water where the pigeons and blackbirds came to drink. How could I not have seen it before? That house was visible from every point in the city. At the end of the streets, above the tumult of cars and humans, stood that white house, majestic, eternal, infinitely contemplating the sun and following its course from one end of the sea to the other.

I walked slowly, cautiously closer, as if time had stopped, as if death and suffering were still in the sumptuous apartments, in the symmetrical park, under the bowers, behind every plaster statue. Walking slowly through the park, I heard the gravel crunching under the soles of my sandals and in that silent domain the noise seemed to make a sharp, compact, almost threatening sound. I thought of the Excelsior Hotel that I saw yesterday near the train station, its gardens, its white baroque façade, its wide entrance adorned with plaster cherubs through which the Jews had to pass before being interrogated. But in the quiet and luxury of the large park, beneath the windows of the white house, despite the cooing of turtledoves and the cries of blackbirds, a deathly silence reigned. I walked on and I could still hear my father's voice in the kitchen of our house in Saint-Martin as he talked about the cellars in which people were killed and tortured every day, cellars hidden under the sumptuous edifice and at night, the screams of women being beaten, the screams of the tormented, muffled by the shrubs and the pools, the shrill screams that one couldn't mistake for the cries of blackbirds, and so perhaps in order not to understand in those days, one had to plug up his ears. I walked along under the high windows of the palace, the windows from which the Nazi officers leaned to observe the streets of the city through binoculars. I used to hear my father uttering the name of the house, The Hermitage, almost every evening I heard him say that name in the dark kitchen when the windows were stopped up with newspaper because of the curfew. And the name remained within me all this time, like a hated secret, The Hermitage, the name that doesn't mean anything to others, signifies nothing other than the big luxury apartments overlooking the sea, the peaceful park crowded with pigeons. I walked around in front of the house looking at the façade, window after window, and the dark mouths of basement windows from where the voices of the tortured rose. There was no one around that day, and despite the sunlight and the sea shining in the distance between the palm trees, a cold shudder arose from deep inside of me.

The Sunday after Elizabeth's death I took the bus to the village of Saint-Martin. In the street with the stream, I looked for the door to our house, a little below street level, with its three or four stone steps leading down. But everything was foreign now, or maybe I'm a foreigner. The stream that bounded down the middle of the narrow street, that was once powerful and dangerous as a river, is but a thin trickle washing a few papers along. The cellars, the old stables are restaurants, pizzerias, ice-cream stands and souvenir shops. In the square there is a new, anonymous building. I even looked for the mysterious, disquieting hotel in front of which my mother and father and I stood in line every morning to have our names checked in the carabinieri's register. The place where Rachel had danced with the Italian officer, where the carabinieri moved poor Mr. Ferne's piano. I ended up realizing that it was the modest two-star hotel with advertisements on the parasols and strange old-fashioned curtains in the windows. Even Mr. Ferne's house—the villa with the mulberry tree—so old and abandoned, where he played Hungarian waltzes just for himself on his black piano, has now become a vacation home. But I did recognize the old mulberry tree. Standing on my tiptoes, I picked a lovely dark green, finely serrated leaf.

I went down below the village till I reached the curve from where you can see the torrent and the dark gorge where we used to go swimming as if in the depths of a secret valley, and once again, I felt all the hairs on my skin bristling with the icy water and the hot sun, and I heard the buzzing of the wasps, and on my chest Tristan's smooth cheek lay as he listened to the beating of my heart. Maybe I heard the laughter of the children, the shrill cries of the girls the boys were splashing, the voices calling, just as before, "Maryse! Sonia!" It made my heart sink and I walked quickly back up to the village.

I wasn't bold enough to speak with anyone. At any rate the old people were dead, the young had all gone. It has all undoubtedly been forgotten. In the narrow streets tourists strolled with their children, their dogs. In the old house where the women lit the lights for Shabbat, there was now a garage. In the square, where the Jews gathered before they struck out walking through the mountains while the troops of the Fourth Italian Army went back up the valley and abandoned the village to the Germans, I saw people playing boules, a Belgian ice-cream parlor. Only the fountain continues to flow, as in the old days, spitting water out of its four mouths for the children who come to drink standing on the edge of the basin.

Since I had no choice, I hitchhiked on the road to Notre-Dame-des-Fenestres. A car driven by a young blond girl stopped. Inside there was a dark young man who looked Italian, and another girl, very dark, with pretty green eyes. In a few minutes the car climbed the road through the forest of larches to the sanctuary. Calmly, I watched the road along which we'd walked, Elizabeth and I, I tried in vain to catch a glimpse of the clearing where we'd slept near the torrent. The young people in the car attempted to talk to me. The young man said something like, "Is this the first time you've come here?" I said no, it wasn't the first time, I'd come once a very long time ago. At the end of the road, above the ring of mountains, the peaks were already hidden in the clouds.

The buildings in which we'd slept, the Italian soldiers' barracks, the chapel, everything was there, but it was as if something had been removed, as if they no longer had the same meaning. In the building we'd slept in, facing the solders' barracks, there was now an Alpine Club Refuge. As a matter of fact, that is where the young people put their bags for the night. For a second I felt like staying with them, sleeping there, but it wasn't possible. "Even in this season you have to reserve a bed at least a week in advance," said the guardian of the refuge to me, looking indifferent. They didn't used to be so picky!

Since it was already late, I didn't feel up to walking on the stone path the tourists took back. So I sat down on the embankment, not far from the barracks, sheltered from the wind by a low stone wall and I looked out at the mountain, at the very place I used to watch until my eyes burned and I shook with dizziness when I was waiting for my father who was supposed to join us. But now I know that he can't come.

The same day my mother and I started out on the road to Italy, my father was escorting a group of fugitives on the path to the border, up above Berthemont. Around noon the Germans took them by surprise. "Duck! Run!" the man from the Gestapo shouted. But as they tried to flee through the tall grass, a spray of machine gun fire cut them down and they fell, one on top of the other, men, women, old people, young children. It was a young woman who hid in the bushes and later in an abandoned sheepfold who told us that, and that's why Elizabeth came back to France, to be in the land where her husband died. She wrote it all down in a single, long letter, on the pages of a school notebook in her fine and elegant hand. She wrote the name of my father, Michel Grève, and the names of all the men and all the women who died with him in the grass, above Berthemont. Now, she too is dead in this same land and her body is closed up in a steel cylinder that I carry around with me.

I walked a ways on the road, in the direction of Saint-Martin. I could hear the peaceful sound of the torrent and the rumblings of the storm behind me in the ring of clouds. Some English tourists picked me up in their car and took me to the village. Despite the tourist season I managed to find a small room in a hotel at the bottom of Rue Central in an old house I wasn't familiar with.

I wanted to see the place my father had died in Berthemont after all. Early the next morning I took the bus to the fork in the road and I walked down to the bottom of the valley till I reached the old abandoned hotel where the thermal baths used to be. I followed the stairway up over the sulfurous torrent, then the path that winds up the mountain. The sky was magnificent. I thought Philip and Michel would have liked to see that, the morning light shining on the grassy slopes, on the rocks. On the other side of the Vesubie valley, the tall blue mountains seemed as light as clouds.

It had been so long since I'd listened to that silence, felt that serenity. I thought of the sea, the way I had seen it one morning when I stuck my head out of the hold of the *Sette Fratelli*, so long ago now that it seems like a legend. I imagined my father being on that boat, just when the sun brushes against the edge of the world and lights up the crests of the waves. That was how he used to talk of Jerusalem, the city of light, as if it were a cloud, or a mirage over a new land. Where is that city? Does it really exist?

I stopped on the side of the mountain, in the place where the huge fields of grass begin and where Mario looked for vipers, the place where I used to dream I'd see my father walking. The sun was beating down, gleaming up in the center of the sky, gathering the shadows into small piles.

The valley was still in the misty half-lit morning, there was not a human shape, not a house, not a sound. The grassy slope rose skyward, as if into infinity. The sole trace, the path.

Now I realized: it was here they had walked, my father leading, the fugitives behind him, in single file, women wrapped in their shawls, children whining or indifferent, and the men in the rear, carrying the suitcases, the sacks of provisions, the woolen blankets. My heart racing, I climbed on through the tall grass. It was the end of summer, just like forty years ago, I remembered it perfectly: the vast sky, so blue, as if you could see the depths of space. The smell of burning grasses, the shrill chirping of crickets. Up above the dark valleys, kites circling, puling. My heart beat faster because I was nearing the truth. It was all there, I hadn't forgotten, it was only yesterday when we walked, my mother and I, on the path of sharp stones, through the storm clouds, toward Italy. The women were sitting on the edge of the path, their bundles on the ground next to them, their eyes staring fixedly into space. The smell of the grass up on the slopes makes your head spin, the way a strong perfume does, maybe the farmers in the village had cut it and it was beginning to ferment. Sweat streamed down my face as I followed the path toward the top of the grassy slope. Then I was in an immense prairie that stretched all the way out to the rocky peaks. I was so high up that I could no longer see the valley bottom. The sun had gone back down toward the blue mountains on the opposite slope. The clouds were puffy, magnificent, I could hear thunder rumbling somewhere.

The shepherd's shelters were just ahead. Ageless drystone huts. Maybe they were already there before men built their cities, their temples, their citadels. As I drew near the shelters, a trembling sort of feeling rose inside of me, despite the hot sun and the heady smell of the tall fermenting grasses. Suddenly I knew, I was sure of it. This was the place. They were hiding there in the stone huts. When the fugitives came up onto the prairie, the killers came out, their machine guns on their hips, someone shouted in French, "Run! Quick, quick, run! Get away, we won't hurt you!" It was a man from the Gestapo who had shouted that, he was wearing an elegant gray suit, with a felt hat on his head. Through the tall grasses the women and children started to run, the old women, the men, like so many panic-stricken animals. Then the S.S. pulled the trigger, and the machine guns raked over the grassy field, bringing the bodies down one on top of the other, and the shrill frightened screams were drowned in blood. Others were still alive, men trying to flee to the bottom of the slope along the path they'd come up on, but the bullets hit them in the back. The bundles, suitcases, sacks of flour fell into the grass, clothes, shoes were strewn about, as if in a game. The soldiers left the bundles. They dragged the bodies by the legs up to the shepherds' huts, and they left them there in the sunlight.

In the evening, rain began to fall on the grassy slope, the stone huts. The path led down through the tall grasses toward the valley deep in shadow, just like another time when the sharp blades came up to my lips and I didn't know where I was anymore. No one goes up there now. Maybe at the end of summer the flocks of sheep led by an old deaf man who talks to his dog, whistling, and sits on a rock to watch the clouds scud over the sky.

I came down the mountain at a near run, through the tall grasses on the slippery path. Do vipers still become entangled in amorous combat? Does anyone still know how to call to them, like Mario, whistling gently between his teeth? Everything was wheeling around me, as if I were the only living creature, the last woman to have escaped war. Then it struck me that Jerusalem—the city of light that my father dreamt of seeing—was up there, on that grassy slope, with all of its celestial domes and the minarets that link the earthly world to the clouds.

In the valley, the night was warm. The rain ran over the road with a soft whisper. A truck driven by an Italian brought me back to Nice. I found what I'd come looking for. In two days Philip and Michel will be here. I love them. I'll go back with them across the sea to my country where the light is so beautiful. It shines most of all in the eyes of the children, the eyes from which I hope to drive all suffering. I know that everything will begin now. And I still think of Nejma, the sister I lost so long ago in the cloud of dust on the path, and whom I must find again.

The sea is beautiful in the twilight. The water, the land, the sky melt into one another. A haze is hovering, shrouding the horizon imperceptibly. And the silence, despite the moving cars, despite the city-dwellers' footsteps. Everything is calm on the breakwater where Esther sits. She stares out to sea, almost without blinking. She's been coming to this place for several days, when the sun descends, to look at the sea. Tonight is the last time. Tomorrow, Philip and Michel will be here and they'll all take the train for Paris, for London together. They must go away, to forget.

Each evening at the same time the fishermen come out to set up their lines. On the slabs of cement making up the breakwater they carefully prepare the bait, the poles, the reels, they work with precise and sure gestures. Esther enjoys watching them. They are so busy, so meticulous, it's as if all other things were only dreams, delusions, the imagination of a madman rambling in the halls of his asylum. So Esther thinks that is what reality is, these fishermen in the twilight, the lines that they now cast into the sea, the weights that whistle as they lash the slack waves, and the mirroring of the light as the swollen sun vanishes in the haze. Esther's gaze wanders in the blue-gray vastness before her, then it focuses on a small lone boat, a thin, lone triangular sail slowly traversing the haze.

Once again it is the end of summer. Days are shorter, night falls abruptly. Esther shivers, in spite of the warm air. Out on the breakwater the fishermen have turned on a radio. The music drifts over in snatches on the wind, a woman's voice singing loudly—it sounds off-key—and the crackling static due to thunderstorms in the mountains.

The fishermen turn around from time to time, seeming to jeer, they say things in the dialect spoken around Nice and she suspects they're talking about her because they laugh a little. Some are young men, the same age as her son, very dark, Italian-looking, with pink short-sleeved shirts. What could they be saying about her? She has a hard time imagining what it might be, dressed as she is, like a vagabond, her short-cropped graying hair, her still-childish face, tanned from days in the sun, in the mountains. But in a way, she's glad to hear their voices, their raucous music, and their laughter. It proves that they are real, that all of this exists, the slow sea, the blocks of cement, the sail moving through the haze. They aren't going to disappear. She feels overwhelmed by the lightness of the air, the luminous haze. The sea with its ebb and flow, its bursts of refracted light, has entered her body. It's the time of day when everything vacillates, is transformed. It's been such a long time since she's known such serenity, such detachment. She remembers the deck of the boat in the night when both the earth and time had ceased to exist. It was after Livorno, or maybe farther south, nearing the Strait of Messina. Disregarding the Captain's order, Esther climbed the ladder and went out the half-open hatch, then she'd crawled over the deck in the cold wind as cautiously as a thief till she reached the front lookout post. Sylvio was on watch and he'd let her by without saying anything, as if he hadn't seen her. Esther remembers now how the boat slipped over the smooth sea, invisible in the night, she remembers the gentle sound of the prow, the tremor of the motors under the deck. In the forecastle, the radio was on and the sailors were listening to a tinny and sputtering tune, the same kind that the fishermen are listening to now. It was the radio for Americans in Sicily, in Tangier, the jazz music broke through the night in wafts, as it does now, we didn't know where we were going, lost in space. It drifted away, came back, the powerful, husky voice of Billie Holiday singing "Solitude" and "Sophisticated Lady", Ada Brown, Jack Dupree, Little Johnnie Jones's fingers on the piano. It was Jacques Berger who had taught her the names, later, when they listened to the records on an old phonograph, in Nora's room in Ramat Yohanan. Esther remembers the song—she sang it in a low voice whenever she went walking around in the streets—and everything she'd discovered in Canada, the music in the apartment on Avenue Notre-Dame that helped her live through the cold and the loneliness of her exile. Now, out on the breakwater, facing the darkening sea, she still floats along on the music coming from the fishermen's radio. She remembers what it was like back then, heading for the unknown across the sea. But she feels a pang in her heart because it occurs to her that for Elizabeth none of that exists anymore, there will be no more journeys. The ship stopped slipping over the sea, borne along on Billie Holiday's music when Elizabeth stopped breathing. She died during the night, alone in her cot, with no one to hold her hand. Esther went into the room and saw her face—so very white, tilted backward on the pillow, the dark stains on her eyelids. She bent over the cold, hard body and she said, "Please, not now. Stay a little longer! I want to talk to you about Italy, about Amantea." She said that in a loud voice, squeezing the cold hand, to let a little warmth into the dead fingers. The nurse came in, she just stood by the door saying nothing.

Now all of that is fading away. It's as if it were in another world, a world where the light was different, where everything had a different color, a different taste, where voices said other things; where eyes held a different look. Her father's voice saying her name, like this: Estrellita, little star; Mr. Ferne's voice, the children's voices shouting in the square in Saint-Martin, Tristan's voice, Rachel's voice, Jacques Berger's voice when he translated the words of Reb Joel in the Toulon prison. Nora's voice, Lola's voice. It's dreadful, the voices that fade away. Now that it is dark, for the first time in years, ever since she'd ceased being a child, Esther feels tears that can come. They spill from her eyes and roll down her cheeks. She doesn't know why she's crying. When Jacques died in the hills of Tiberias, three soldiers came to the kibbutz bearing the news, two men and a woman. They said, as if they were excusing themselves, Jacques Berger died on January 10, he was buried. They left right away. They had very gentle faces.

Esther hadn't cried then. Maybe there had been no tears in her at the time, because of the war. Maybe it was because of the sunlight on the fields, in the groves, the light that clung to Yohanan's black hair, because of the silence and the bright sky. Now she feels the tears come as if the sea were rising into her eyes.

From the bag she's carried around for days through the streets of the city and up in the mountains on the grassy slope where her father died, Esther takes the metal cylinder with the ashes inside. With all her might she twists off the cover. The wind blowing over the blocks of cement is warm, it comes in gusts, bringing with it the sound of the tinny music, it quite resembles Billie Holiday's voice singing "Solitude"0 over near the Messina Strait. But it must surely be something else. The wind and the night sieze the ashes spilling from the metallic canister, scatter them seaward. At times an eddy brings the ashes back to Esther, blinding her, dusting her hair with them. When the canister is empty,

Esther throws it far away, and the splash in the sea makes the fishermen turn their heads. Then she closes the bag and jumps from block to block along the jetty. She walks along the wharves. She feels immensely weary, immensely serene. There are bats dancing around the lampposts.

J. M. G. LE CLÉZIO is a distinguished, French author with over 30 novels, essays, and story collections to his credit. He was born in Nice in 1940, and after completing his undergraduate degree in literature at the University of Nice, he continued his studies in England. His first novel, *Le Procès-Verbal*, was published in 1963. In 2008, he was awarded the Nobel Prize in Literature. Since the 1990s, Le Clézio and his wife have shared their time between Albuquerque, New Mexico, the island of Mauritius, and Nice, France.

CURBSTONE PRESS, INC.

is a nonprofit publishing house dedicated to literature that reflects a commitment to social change, with an emphasis on contemporary writing from Latino, Latin American and Vietnamese cultures. Curbstone presents writers who give voice to the unheard in a language that goes beyond denunciation to celebrate, honor and teach. Curbstone builds bridges between its writers and the public – from inner-city to rural areas, colleges to community centers, children to adults. Curbstone seeks out the highest aesthetic expression of the dedication to human rights and intercultural understanding: poetry, testimonies, novels, stories, and children's books.

This mission requires more than just producing books. It requires ensuring that as many people as possible learn about these books and read them. To achieve this, a large portion of Curbstone's schedule is dedicated to arranging tours and programs for its authors, working with public school and university teachers to enrich curricula, reaching out to underserved audiences by donating books and conducting readings and community programs, and promoting discussion in the media. It is only through these combined efforts that literature can truly make a difference.

Curbstone Press, like all nonprofit presses, depends on the support of individuals, foundations, and government agencies to bring you, the reader, works of literary merit and social significance which might not find a place in profit-driven publishing channels, and to bring the authors and their books into communities across the country. Our sincere thanks to the many individuals, foundations, and government agencies who have supported this endeavor: Connecticut Commission on the Arts, Connecticut Humanities Council, Eastern CT Community Foundation, Fisher Foundation, Greater Hartford Arts Council, Hartford Courant Foundation, J. M. Kaplan Fund, Lamb Family Foundation, Lannan Foundation, John D. and Catherine T. MacArthur Foundation, National Endowment for the Arts, Open Society Institute, Puffin Foundation, United Way, and the Woodrow Wilson National Fellowship Foundation.

Please help to support Curbstone's efforts to present the diverse voices and views that make our culture richer. Tax-deductible donations can be made by check or credit card to:
Curbstone Press, 321 Jackson Street, Willimantic, CT 06226
phone: (860) 423-5110 fax: (860) 423-9242
www.curbstone.org

IF YOU WOULD LIKE TO BE A MAJOR SPONSOR OF A
CURBSTONE BOOK, PLEASE CONTACT US.